#3
VIRGIN TERRITORY
BY E. J. HUNTER

ZEBRA BOOKS
KENSINGTON PUBLISHING CORP.

ZEBRA BOOKS

are published by

KENSINGTON PUBLISHING CORP.
475 Park Avenue South
New York, N.Y. 10016

Copyright © 1984 by E. J. Hunter

All rights reserved. No part of this book may be reproduced in any form or by any means without the prior written consent of the Publisher, excepting brief quotes used in reviews.

Second printing: January 1986

Printed in the United States of America

ALLEY CAT CHASE

"There she is. I don't believe it, but there, see her over by the church," Jake Tulley whispered excitedly to Luke Wellington.

The rangy blond gunhawk peered down from the balcony of the Hotel Le Provencial at the throng and recognized the trim form of Rebecca Caldwell, despite the stylish clothing she wore. "You're right, boss."

"Take three of the boys and go get her. We haven't time to wait around for Roger's fancy ideas to work out."

"Right away."

Even in a crowd, the lessons she had learned living with the Oglala set a warning going in Rebecca's mind. Faces that didn't belong. That impression registered first. Two men, headed in her direction, worked their way through the clots of people with determination. Their fixed expressions further alarmed her. She turned away from them and started to ease a path through the chattering women and bartering vendors. A quick glance showed that the men altered direction to match hers. She started walking faster, her right hand tightly gripped the butt of the Baby Russian in her purse. A darkly shaded alleyway on the east side of the square caught her attention.

A plan formed as she headed toward the narrow opening. . . .

WHITE SQUAW
Zebra's Adult Western Series
by E.J. Hunter

#1: SIOUX WILDFIRE	(1205, $2.50)
#2: BOOMTOWN BUST	(1286, $2.50)
#3: VIRGIN TERRITORY	(1314, $2.50)
#4: HOT TEXAS TAIL	(1359, $2.50)
#5: BUCKSKIN BOMBSHELL	(1410, $2.50)
#6: DAKOTA SQUEEZE	(1479, $2.50)
#7: ABILENE TIGHT SPOT	(1562, $2.50)
#8: HORN OF PLENTY	(1649, $2.50)
#9: TWIN PEAKS — OR BUST	(1746, $2.50)

Available wherever paperbacks are sold, or order direct from the Publisher. Send cover price plus 50¢ per copy for mailing and handling to Zebra Books, Dept. 1314, 475 Park Avenue South, New York, N.Y. 10016. DO NOT SEND CASH.

Dedicated to all modern women, who pioneer in the fields of business, industry, medicine and literature. May you press on to your goals.

"Annie Mc** had lagged behind, walking, when we stopped. The whole train crossed the creek before they thought of her. . . . We hear many stories of Indian depredations . . ."

—Jane Gould Tortillott
Diary of the Westward Journy.

CHAPTER 1

Amy Branson sat under the fluttering, pale green leaves of an ancient, gnarled cottonwood tree. The warm, Nebraska breeze ruffled the silky strands of her long, blonde hair and the russet yarn locks of her favorite doll. She sang to herself as she worked the cotton batting-stuffed arms into the sleeves of another dress, the sixth her dolly had been subjected to that bright sunny morning.

"Green cof-fee grows on white oak tops . . ." Her voice, high, thin and pure, carried across the farmyard of her father's homestead. In the distance, crows provided a harmony and fat, sleek cows lowed in the corral, feeding contentedly after their morning milking. Life couldn't be better, Amy thought, for any girl only three months from her twelfth birthday. Her contentment knew no possibility that it might be worse.

Amy looked up from her play at the sound of horses hoofs.

Three men rode into the farmyard. *Indians,* Amy saw with a slight chill. They wore hunting shirts, leggings and the usual trappings of the Sioux. Friendly braves frequently visited, to barter for sugar and coffee beans, so her unease came only from childish fantasies. She gave a friendly wave and returned to dressing a second doll. Then the chilling fantasies turned into reality.

"Grab her," a harsh voice commanded in English.

Two of the riders dismounted and hurried to where Amy squatted under the cottonwood. They carried thin ropes and one held a wad of dirty cloth.

"Come on, little girlie, you're going with us."

"No!" Amy shouted. "Stay away from me. Poppa! Help me, Poppa!"

She tried to run, but to no avail. The lanky, rangy men caught her easily and bent her arms behind her. She struggled, yelling for help all the while, and their strong fingers hurt her delicate skin. Even though she twisted her head from side to side, one of the strangers managed to force the gag into her mouth. Amy kicked him and tried to break free. Then she caught sight of her father, coming from the barn with a shotgun in his hands.

"Hey, you, get away from her," Carl Branson demanded. He raised his Parker and smoke belched from the muzzle of the righthand barrel.

Amy heard the man who remained on horseback grunt and what sounded like hail rip through the leaves overhead. Shreds of green trickled down on her head while one of the men tied her hands. The other bent to her flailing ankles while the rider drew his revolver.

The shot sounded loud to Amy and she shrieked soundlessly in horror when she saw her father fall down.

"Hurry up," the man growled. "We got to get outta here."

The other men threw Amy roughly to the ground and secured her ankles, then tossed her over the pommel of a saddle. Quickly they mounted and rode out of the clearing. The last thing Amy heard was her mother's frightened cries from far behind. Then she lost consciousness.

Flames crackled from the wooden upper story of the soddy. A woman screamed from inside and a man's deeper tones sounded in a rude laugh.

"Hurry up and fuck her, Red, then we'll stick an arrah in her and git out of here. This thing's gonna burn down around our ears in a little while."

"You don't want any?"

"Sure. Drag her outside, then."

Red pulled the struggling woman out by her feet and hoisted her dress under the shade of a small elm tree. Two small, blonde girls shrieked in terror at the sight and renewed their desperate sobs. Not far away the corpses of a man and two boys, one in his teens, lay sprawled in death. The men, who spoke in English, wore the clothing of Oglala Sioux warriors. They quickly went about their rape of the farmwife.

"Loosen up, lady an' give me some help," Red complained as he forced his rigid organ into her dry, resisting passage. "You like it," the marauder went on, "you know you do . . . or you wouldn't have four kids."

"Move it, Red. It's my turn."

"Shut up, Marv. This is like fuckin' a sand pit," Red growled.

Three other men tied the girls' hands behind them

and fastened their legs together with other rawhide strips. Then they chucked them into the back of a covered buckboard. The leader called out to the rapists.

"Git a move on, Red, Marv. We ain't got all day."

When the buckboard pulled out, the two little blonde girls whimpered and wondered why the world had so suddenly gone awful for them.

White canvas tops, like the sails of mighty schooners, spread in a line across the vast prairie. Men armed with many weapons rode along the flanks and others, with a variety of firearms in profusion, rode the seats of the Conestogas and other, smaller conveyances. At a closer distance, the high voices of children could be heard from under the coverings. The sounds they made were mournful, rather than the shrill shouts of joyful youth. At the head of the wagon train, astride a barrel-chested roan, a hard-faced woman rode beside the wagon master. From time to time she spat a brown stream of tobacco juice into the waving buffalo grass. As the long string of vehicles rolled along, she first consulted the sun, then a large turnip pocket watch she pulled from her whipcord trousers.

"Circle 'em up for the night," she ordered, then turned back to the lead wagon.

"Right, Hattie," the wagon master sent over his shoulder to her.

Within fifteen minutes, the seven vehicles had been closed into a ring and a large cookfire burned near the chuckwagon. Ten young girls, uniformly blonde and blue-eyed, came from their confinement under canvas and began routine chores in a listless manner. Several bore the marks of recent punishment, mostly bruises on their cheeks or arms.

"All right, little ladies," Hattie Ketridge informed her charges in a cawing voice. "Any of you got to squat and pee, you'll do it with a guard watching. No more of these sneaky attempts to get away."

"Y-you mean with . . . with a *man* watching us?" one small, timid voice inquired.

"Why, hell yes, honey. It ain't gonna be long before a *man* is gonna do more'n look at that li'll muff between yer legs. So why not get used to it now? An' remember, boys," she went on to the gathered hardcases, "you can look, but don't touch. The merchandise has to be delivered in a whole condition." She emitted a harsh bray of laughter at her bad pun.

"Hold up, there," a sentry's voice called from outside the circle of wagons. "Oh, it's you, Clyde. How many'd ya get?"

"Only two. This one's paw," he pointed down at Amy Branson draped over his saddle, "put a couple o' buckshot pellets in my shoulder."

"Amos'll patch that up. Ride on in. Supper will be ready shortly."

"What do we have here?" Hattie brayed at the new arrivals.

"Two more gals, Miss Hattie. Prime stuff, I'd allow."

"Good work, Clyde. Now you go over to the chuckwagon an' have Amos dig them pellets out. I'll take care of these."

The two girls had been dumped on the ground and Hattie bent over them, a thin-bladed sheath knife in one hand. She cut free the bindings at their wrists and ankles and roughly stood them on their feet.

"You ain't gonna make a bunch of silly noises if I take them gags out, are you?" she demanded of them.

Frightened and fatigued, Amy and the other girl shook their heads.

"Good then." Hattie removed the gags.

"What . . . why are you doing this?" Amy asked in an unsteady voice.

"Well, now, that's for us to know and you to find out, ain't it? An' the first thing you're gonna find out is that we don't brook no smart-ass questions, young miss." She reached out and grabbed flesh on Amy's chest, where the first swelling of childish breasts had begun to show. Powerful fingers clamped down and Hattie gave a vicious twist to her pinch. Pain tears welled in Amy's eyes.

"That's what you can expect any time you get wise-mouthed around here," Hattie informed her. "The both of you had better learn to behave right now. To make it clear, you can go to your beds without supper. Over there, in that . . . ah, third wagon. Now, git!"

Another girl sat on a large pillow in the wagon box. "I'm Lisa," she introduced herself when the frightened, confused youngsters clambered over the tailgate. "You're being punished like all of us the first night."

"I'm Amy Branson," Amy returned.

"I'm Flora Carson," the other new captive said.

"What is all this? Why have they stolen us from our homes?" Amy demanded in a rush.

"Don't you know?" Lisa countered, eyes big and rolling in her heart-shaped face. "The way I figure it, from hearin' Miss Hattie talk—that's her, the one who pinches, Miss Hattie Ketridge—we're being taken south to Texas. They're gonna put us in one of them whoorhouses so the cowboys can stick their things in us."

Amy gave her an uncomprehending, blank stare.

"You know. Down here," she pointed to her crotch. "I ain't never done it yet, but I seen my older sister an' our cousin Roddy in the barn once. He had this stiff red thing pokin' out that he shoved down between Sally's legs, then they began slammin' their hips together. It must feel good 'cause Sally squealed a lot while they were doin' it. Then Roddy shivered and grunted like the pigs when they're doin' it and lay still on top of Sally. It made me itch and get all wet watchin'. An' I was only nine then."

"What happened to your sister? Is she here?"

"Naw. When those men came to steal us, they found out she had done it a few times so they all poked her good. Then . . . They . . . they killed her." Big tears appeared in Lisa's eyes. "S-she was o-only fourteen an' now she's dead."

"That's awful," Flora exclaimed.

Lisa reached out and embraced Flora. One hand gently stroked the girl's blonde locks. "Don't worry, little Flora, I'll watch out for you."

"What's going to happen to us?" Amy inquired.

"Oh, Miss Hattie's gonna poke her finger up inside of you to make sure everything is like it oughtta be. Other than that, everyone sorta leaves us alone?"

"Really?" Amy asked with a quick intake of breath.

"I . . . ever since those men took me away, I've been thinking that if I could once get loose, I'd run away."

"Me, too," Flora added.

"They don't keep us tied, do they?" Amy went on.

"No," Lisa told her.

"Then . . . we can do it. Oh, Lisa, do you want to?"

"Yes. We can sneak off in the night some time," Lisa responded.

The girls talked on until after dark. Tired and sore, Amy and Flora fell asleep soon after that. Quietly, Lisa slipped out of the wagon and went to where Hattie Ketridge sat by the fire drinking whiskey-laced coffee. Lisa gave the horse-faced woman a shy peck on the cheek and made her report.

"I told them the same story, like all the new girls. They both talked about running off. I don't know when, but I'll tell you what I learn."

Hattie smiled, a vulture contemplating a feast of rotted flesh. She offered the twelve-year-old a sip of her coffee. "That's a good girl, Lisa. You did well." She brushed her stubby-fingered hand caressingly across the child's budding breasts.

"We'll be in Kansas before noon," Lone Wolf told Rebecca Caldwell as they made camp in the lingering prairie twilight.

"Good. I'm positive Jake Tulley has left Colorado," the attractive young girl replied. She ran graceful long fingers through her raven hair and peered off eastward with keen, clear blue eyes. Kansas. Maybe there she would catch up with Bitter Creek Jake Tulley and his gang of reprobates, highwaymen and drygulchers. Five long years of her life had been stolen by Tulley and her worthless uncles, Ezekial and Virgil Caldwell.

Five years captive of the Sioux. Wife to an Oglala warrior, then widow and married again to yet another Indian. All because of the Tulley gang. She had been only fourteen when, to save their own worthless hides, Jake Tulley and her uncles bartered some old guns, a case of whiskey and Rebecca and her mother, Hannah, off to Iron Calf, a powerful Oglala war chief.

Her greatest shock came when, rather than being raped to death by the lusty braves, she and her mother were put under the protection of Iron Calf. By the time she discovered that she was in fact daughter to Iron Calf, she had gone beyond shocks or surprises.

In her youth, Hannah Caldwell had been raped by an Oglala brave, whose identity she did not know. Rebecca had been the product of that brief union. Years later Hannah discovered that Rebecca's father was Iron Calf, then the leader of a large band of Oglala that made their camp some thirty miles from the Caldwell farm. She kept that secret, even during their terrible captivity. Hannah's mind had mercifully fled her and she received the special privileged position the Sioux reserved for the deranged. Rebecca, however, maintained an all too clear image of those five years. Gradually it became replaced with a new vision.

She lived and survived among the Sioux for only one purpose. To hunt down Bitter Creek Jake Tulley and kill him, along with everyone responsible for her captivity among her father's people. She didn't hate him, or the Oglala. The heat that burned in her soul had turned against the outlaw leader and his men. And especially her uncles.

Virgil had already paid the price for his perfidy, shot through the head by Rebecca. Ezekial nearly did, and carried a bullet in his arm, one fired by his niece, which she intended for his heart.

"One day, I'll get them all."

"What?"

Rebecca didn't realize she had spoken aloud the vow her reflections had renewed. "I . . . I was just thinking about Tulley."

"Do you ever think of anything else?" Lone Wolf asked. His blond hair and gray eyes belied his name. Born Bret Baylor, the man known as Lone Wolf had himself endured years of captivity, but among the Crows, deadly enemies of the Sioux. He had proven himself to his captors and become a famous warrior. Like Rebecca, he came to prefer the comfortable, practical clothing of the Indians over the restrictive dress of white folk. On a raid against the Oglala, Lone Wolf had encountered Rebecca and they decided to escape their savage captors together. Since then they had ridden as fast companions on Rebecca's quest against Tulley and his gang. Lone Wolf had only recently removed the emblem of his warrior society, the tall, bristly roach hair style that marked him as a Crow Strong Heart. Now a faint fuzz could be seen over his entire bald pate. Before long he would have less distinctive looks. Ike, Rebecca's big stallion, snorted, alerting them both.

"Someone coming," Rebecca declared.

"Quietly, too. Could be the Oglala, looking for you."

They had encountered several parties of young men from Iron Calf's band in the past. All had been charged with tracking down Rebecca and returning her. Most died in the attempt. Now the undaunted pair waited tensely to learn the identity of their visitor.

"Hello at the fire," a voice called from a screen of tall sagebrush some fifty yards from camp. The man spoke in accented Lakota. "I come bearing the beads of peace."

"Come forward then, man of peace. What do you want with us?" Rebecca answered fluently in the Sioux language.

A tall, handsome warrior, dressed in the manner of the Cheyenne, appeared at the side of the cluster of sage. He held his right hand upward, a wide strip of tanned deer hide, ornately decorated with over a hundred rows of beads, dangling from the open palm. He did not answer until he led his pony up to the picket line alongside Rebecca and Lone Wolf's mounts and their pack horse. He looped the rawhide reins over the length of rope and came forward again, extending his "safe passage" belt of wampum.

"I am called Sure Knife of the Natawa *Sahiela*." he introduced himself, using the Sioux name for the Cheyenne. "I am seeking the woman known by her Oglala brothers as *Sinaskawin*. Are you that one?"

"I am," Rebecca acknowledged.

Sure Knife nodded with satisfaction. "Then I have a piece of paper with the white man's marks on it for you. It comes from a friend of yours, Swift Doe, who is living among the whites now."

"Yes. I know her." She recalled her last encounter with Swift Doe. The Oglala girl's boisterous greeting in the streets of Jury Wells had nearly cost Rebecca her life. What did she want now?

The Cheyenne warrior handed her a carefully folded and preserved piece of paper which he took from inside his buckskin hunting shirt.

Rebecca opened the letter and looked at the words on it. "White Robe Girl, this is Swift Doe, talking to you through the speaking marks of Doctor Lewis in Jury Wells. He puts sign pictures on paper of what I say. There is much trouble among the people of Iron Calf's village and other bands of the Oglala. Our brothers are being blamed for something they do not do. White settler girls, those having only nine to fourteen winters, are being stolen from their families. They are being carried off to no one knows where. Our people are being blamed for it.

"You know that there is little use for a white girl in our camps. They must learn everything new, like a baby, and often ruin good robes, are lazy and cry a lot. So even if these girls are taken away it would not be by those who have no use for them. I have seen such young girls in the company of a big white woman who acts like a man and some of the bad whites who rode the white war path with the one you seek, Jake Tulley. They take these girls to a train of rolling wood. The men there have many rifles and all have bad hearts. They chase away Swift Doe and her man, even though he is white like them. The rolling wood has left here over a moon ago. It go in direction of the land of the *Pani*. Where it go from there I do not know. People talk of killing the Oglala, even though there is now peace. Would you, White Robe Girl, please aid your Oglala brothers by learning about the stolen girls?"

Rebecca handed the letter to Lone Wolf. "Did Swift Doe give any other message?" she inquired of the Cheyenne messenger.

"She said to do this thing fast, or many who do nothing wrong will by hurt by the white-eyes. Already two of Sleeping Bull's band have been found shot on the buffalo range. Many more might die."

CHAPTER 2

When Lone Wolf finished reading the letter, he and Rebecca exchanged a silent glance of agreement.

"If Swift Doe saw men who once rode with Jake Tulley, the chances are they are still with him," Rebecca reasoned aloud. "Stealing children has all the markings of a Jake Tulley job." She turned her attention to Sure Knife. "Swift Doe says that the wagon train is headed toward the land of the Pawnee, to the south," she added. "In a month, that could put them somewhere in Kansas. Tell Swift Doe that we will look at this thing."

"Another will take that message," Sure Knife replied. "I must surrender the peace belt, for I have taken up the pipe for my relatives among the Oglala. My wife is of Sleeping Bull's band. Four men of the Dog Soldier society have smoked with me and wait a short ride away. If you take the cause of the Oglala, then we take the warpath with you, *Sinaskawin*."

"We will ride together, but I fight my own way," Rebecca told him. "One thing we must agree upon. Bitter Creek Jake Tulley is mine to kill."

Sure Knife nodded. "It will be so."

* * *

A partly cloudy morning found the five Cheyenne in Rebecca's small camp. They brought with them a haunch of antelope, which Rebecca cooked for breakfast. Afterward, Rebecca changed her accustomed white doeskin dress for the clothes of a white woman. Her Baby Russian went into the velvet clutch purse she carried and a decorous sidesaddle replaced the high pommeled Mexican rig she usually rode. Sure Knife and his Cheyenne blinked in amazement at the transformation.

"It's uncomfortable," she explained, "though it does let me move around in town with more ease. The town of Tribune is not far. We will ride close to it and I will go in alone to ask questions."

More clouds had piled up by the time the seven riders neared Tribune, Kansas. Rebecca studied the sky and estimated that a heavy thunderstorm would develop within several hours, by the next day for certain. She left her companions among some mesquite-shaded sand hills and cantered the final mile into town. A large general mercantile store bore a sign that identified it as the post office. In front, iron posts, sunk deeply into the ground, with a sagging loop of chain between them, served as a tie-rail. Rebecca stopped there, dismounted and entered the clapboarded building.

"Mornin', Ma'am," the proprietor greeted. He worked in a small, metal cage, black sleeve protectors on the arms of his white shirt, a green eyeshade perched on his forehead. He squinted over the tops of wire-rimmed, half-spectacles. "Mail's not up yet."

"I'm not expecting anything," Rebecca answered. "I need some information."

"What about, Ma'am?"

"Have you heard of an unusual wagon train? A lot of heavily armed men escorting it. A lot of children—girls—aboard?"

"Nooo. Can't say as I have. Which way were they headed?"

"South."

"Not the usual thing, that's right." Small black eyes twinkled behind the Franklin glasses. "There'd be talk about such a company, for certain. Sorry I can't help you, Miss."

"I'll ask around a little. Do you have a marshal in town?"

"Yep. He's also the barber. You'll find him in his shop down the street."

"Thank you."

Rebecca left the savory scent of coffee grinder, pickle barrel and bright yellow new rope behind to the outer air, that smelled of dust, heat and a faint hint of approaching rain. A block down the boardwalk, she located the barber shop.

She received no more help there. The marshal, Woody Steinert, had not seen or heard of such a wagon train. Nor had he been informed of it by the law at Goodland to the north or Syracuse to the south. Rebecca thanked him and stepped outside.

"Ah! What is this I perceive?" a rich, vibrant baritone voice exclaimed from behind her. "'*Age cannot wither, nor custom stale her infinite variety. Other women cloy the appetites they feed, while she makes hungry where most she satisfies.*' I must be in the presence of the most lovely woman in Tribune." A tall, markedly handsome young man stepped around in front of Rebecca. He whisked a short, stylish beaver hat from his flowing, wavy brown hair and pressed it over his heart.

"Permit me to introduce myself. I am Jason Millard, thespian, traveler and entrepreneur of a renowned theatrical company, currently stranded in this bountiful city by the contrariness of a broken axle. And you, my dear?"

Rebecca had to suppress a giggle. Jason Millard was really good looking, slender, tall, mesmerizing gray eyes, an intriguing dimple in the point of his chin. "I . . . I'm Rebecca Caldwell."

"Ah, Becky. A most fitting name, Miss Caldwell."

"That was some pretty speech you made. Do you say such things to all of the girls?" Rebecca found herself suddenly flushed with the first tinglings of desire.

"No. Only to the most lovely among all the blossoms. That small quote was from Shakespeare, *Anthony and Cleopatra*. I was comparing your beauty to that of the Queen of the Nile."

Despite her years of living as a Sioux, Rebecca found herself blushing. "Oh, I hardly think I deserve that."

"*Au contraire!* I find you the most radiant bloom in a garden of floral delights. May I offer you tea and cakes?"

Rebecca looked around the chuckholed, dusty single street of Tribune's business district. "In . . . this town?"

"Definitely. I have all the necessaries in my suite at the hotel. Shall we proceed there?"

The tingling had grown to a positive itch and her

heart quickened. "Why . . . why not? Tea and cakes. It's so, ah, Eastern."

Jason smiled. "Continental, my dear. I also have some excellent champagne."

"Lead on, Mr. Jason Millard," Rebecca declared with only a slight tremble in her voice.

Half an hour later, she lay naked on Jason Millard's big brass bed.

With light, teasing strokes the actor trailed his fingers along the delightful curves, hollows and swells of her silken body. Each touch thrilled her anew. His lips nuzzled the hollow of her throat and Rebecca caught her breath, feeling herself moisten in anticipation. Jason had an enormous organ, rigid and pulsing and she circled it with both hands, sliding the brown-tinged skin up and down in a slow, lazy manner.

"You are truly a delight to behold, my dear Becky," Jason murmured.

Rebecca increased the tempo of her strokes as his lips closed over one hardened nipple and his tongue teased its sensitive surface. Passion's dew drops glistened now in the sparse thatch of curly black strands that adorned her cleft, swollen now from adroit manipulation and invitingly open to reveal the pink petals that guarded her portal.

Jason lifted her by her narrow waist and positioned her astraddle his hips. Slowly he lowered the panting girl until the spongy tip of his massive phallus caressed her pulsating mound. His strong arms and hands moved her in languid circles and the nearness of his burning, tumescent flesh teased her into a near frenzy. When she felt she could endure it no longer, Jason plunged her downward and impaled her on his iron-rod member.

She sighed with contentment as her weight bore her down, encompassing more and more of that most wonderful of objects. Rebecca had always had a passionate nature, easily stimulated to arousal, and after her first delicious encounter with Two Horns, her Oglala lover and eventual husband, she could never get enough of this precious sharing of ultimate pleasure.

Her mind soared to the heavens while her body reacted to the marvelous joining. Muscles contracted, encasing the rigid staff deeply within her wildly tingling passage. Oh, if it could go on forever like this, her mind sang.

Jason began to drive into her then, his own excitement making him delirious with joy. None of the many women he had known in his twenty-five years had been quite like this. Becky *liked* making love and did it with a naturalness and abandon that stimulated him beyond all expectations. He felt himself rushing upward to completion and held back, prolonging the sweet agony of their combat of the flesh. Time merged into a whirlpool of sensual grandeur and he came back to reality only at the sound of Rebecca's whimpers.

Eyes glazed, mouth sagging in ardor, Rebecca lashed her head from side to side, panting and groaning as she experienced a long series of mind-numbing peaks that set bright colored lights exploding in her brain. Quickly her ultimate release brought Jason along and he burst within her in a shuddering volley that left them both weak and damp from exertion.

They lay on their sides, still joined by the partially flaccid shaft of flesh that had so delighted her. Rebecca's fingers strayed to its base and began to coax new life from it. She thrilled to its stiffening response and hitched one leg over Jason's firm buttocks, driving him once more into the silken purse that welcomed him with a glissando of small twitches.

Not until they had mounted Olympus for a third remarkable time did they rest. Jason poured champagne.

"What about the tea and cakes?" Rebecca teased.

"I really have them, you know," Jason replied in a distant manner.

"I prefer the sort of nourishment we've just been enjoying," Rebecca responded in a husky voice. She sipped some of the bubbly wine, cool and refreshing against her lips. Then she bent down and took deep into her mouth the now limp creature that had brought her so much happiness. Surprisingly it immediately began to respond. Her busy tongue worked miracles over the broad tip, sending shivers of expectation through both of them. Gradually, as the mighty lance continued to grow, she ingested more of it.

Two hours later, they began to dress in the mid-afternoon glow of the sun through a roller shade.

"Did you find what you came looking for?" Jason inquired.

"No . . . well, yes. In a way I did. Only I didn't learn anything about . . ." caution caused her to pause.

"About what, my lovely Becky?"

"A wagon train. A rather mysterious one that is traveling to somewhere south of here."

"It may have taken a more easterly route," Jason suggested.

"True. Only . . . on the street, shortly before I met you, I saw two men who looked familiar." Rebecca shuddered slightly as she again pictured the rat-like features of Evan Cramer and the tubby body of Charlie Wilks, two hardened killers who rode for Jake Tulley, whom she had encountered in Grub Stake, Colorado. She couldn't have been wrong. She *had* seen them that morning in Tribune.

Rebecca made quick excuses to Jason after thanking him for a delightful afternoon. She felt warm, comforted and satisfied, truly appreciate for all they had shared. She rode out of town to the distant grumble of thunder.

Charlie Wilks stood at the batwing doors to a ratty saloon on the edge of Tribune. He held a half-full mug of beer in one hand and motioned to another man with his other.

"C'mere, Cramer. Take a look."

Evan Cramer joined him. "What is it?"

"That fancy-dressed gal ridin' outta town. If she wasn't so gussied up and looking so at home on that sidesaddle, I'd swear it was that niece of Zeke Caldwell's. The one busted up our big play in Grub Stake."

"Naw. What'd she be here for?" Evan's pointy nose twitched, rodent-like and his small, beady eyes glittered with a natural malevolence. He smoothed his heavily oiled, sleek black hair back on his long head and gulped down a shot of cheap bar whiskey. "You don't think . . . ?

"That's the one thing I don't think, that she's on to us and what we plan to do tomorrow. You sure we can count on this boy you brung in?"

"Bob? No worries with him. He knows his job."

"He'd better. We got a passel of ridin' to do to catch up with Jake and the boys. Bringin' along a little money will make us a big welcome. We don't have time to waste on doin' it more'n once."

"No problem on that score. We'll be in and out with the money like a shot."

"That's what we don't want . . . any shooting."

An hour before sunrise, the storm broke over Tribune. Lightning flashed through the sky and burst apart two of the sparse population of trees in the sandy hills around town. Great sheets of rain fell, turning the narrow, rutted road into a morass of clinging mud. Thunder boomed and rattled and the horses picketed together near Rebecca's camp shrieked in confusion and fear. With all the skill of his Cheyenne ancestors, Sure Knife calmed the wall-eyed beasts.

Day came with no let-up, nearly as dark as night, with huge towers of thunderheads roiling through the tormented air. A fire was impossible. Cold jerky and biscuits made up breakfast. The fury of the tumult made talking out of the question. Rather than abating as time wore on, the tempest increased in power.

Rebecca heard it first, like the rushing, growling sound of a runaway locomotive racing across the plains. Out of the southwest, where the horizon had been tinted an eerie greenish-gray, a dark funnel cloud descended from the black belly of a monstrous cumulo-nimbus and dipped toward the earth. Huge billows of dirt and sprays of water rose around the narrow tip as it touched down and raced toward Tribune. The frightful raging of the whirlwind increased as it drew nearer.

"Tornado," Lone Wolf declared.

The Cheyenne warriors had hidden themselves under buffalo robes, the tremendous storm a symbol to them of the Great Spirit's anger. A wild thrill shared the trembling unease in Rebecca Caldwell's breast as she watched the most destructive of nature's forces at its work of demolition. Faintly, church bells could be heard clanging a warning from Tribune as the rampage raced toward the helpless town.

"They're going to need help if that hits town," Rebecca observed in a shout.

"I'll saddle the horses," Lone Wolf offered.

"Hurry, there's a roof going off now."

CHAPTER 3

"This is one heller of a storm," Bob Tolle remarked from the bar in the small saloon on the edge of Tribune.

"Perfect for what we're plannin'," Charlie Wilks responded.

"When we gonna do it?" Bob asked, anxious to get into action.

"Now's as good a time as any," Evan Cramer decided for them.

Together, the three hardcases left the saloon, heads bent into the raging storm. Their boots made squelching sounds in the muddy street.

The door to the storm cellar behind Milton Hollister's house flew open. Three men stood there. Each held a blue steel Colt revolver. The banker looked up startled, his wife uttered a little shriek and fluttered to the floor. His children looked on wide eyed.

"Out, banker. We got business at yer vault."

"No, I . . ."

"Move it or I put a bullet through one of yer brats. Bob, help the gentleman up the stairs. Then you stay here and keep these folks quiet."

Five minutes later, the two bandits and their hostage banker stopped at the wide double doors of the brick bank building. Hollister nervously fumbled with the keys while lightning split the heavens with crackling fire and a rich odor of ozone filled the streets of Tribune. The wind began to roar louder. At last the lock yielded and the outlaws urged their captive inside.

"Open the safe." Evan Cramer had to shout to be heard. Unseen by the robbers or the banker, the violent funnel cloud of the tornado raced toward town. The noise increased. Dust flew from cracks in the walls and a faint vibration could be felt in the soles of their boots.

"I'll not submit to this sort of treatment," Hollister blustered.

"Open the goddamned safe you fat old toad," Charlie Wilks growled.

"You'll not get away with this."

"Don't try to sound funny," Cramer menaced.

The horses made heavy going against the fury of the tornado that had already struck the fringes of Tribune. Sections of picket fence flew through the boiling air, and a brittle popping could be heard as nails pulled from wooden roofs and walls. An outhouse abruptly took flight, then scattered into a million pieces as its fastenings gave way. Rebecca wiped constantly at her eyes, nearly blinded by the heavy downpour.

"Hurry," she urged.

Hailstones slashed at their exposed skin in stinging balls of ice. Her sturdy stallion, Ike, stumbled once, then regained his footing to struggle on.

"We don't want to get there *before* it hits," Lone Wolf observed judiciously. "What's this all about anyway?"

"There's something . . . not quite right in that town. I have a feeling there's more danger there than the twister."

"Go back to Bob at the house there and bring a couple of the banker's brats," Wilks ordered, an idea forming in his mind.

"Leave my family out of this!" Banker Hollister yelled, eyes shifting around in fright.

"Go on, Ev."

Then the tornado hit.

The bank windows bulged outward and exploded into showers of glittering fragments. Rain and mud blasted into the building and the power of the tortured air ripped at their clothes. Hollister staggered and slammed into the marble-topped divider that formed the teller's cages. He recoiled off it and into the arms of Evan Cramer. The outlaw nearly dropped his revolver.

"Get to that safe," he snarled.

Above them the roof shuddered and threatened to sail off with the clutter of debris already filling the howling maelstrom outside. Down the block, the small wooden structure of Woody Steinert's barber shop ballooned dangerously and then disintegrated into long, deadly slivers of shattered boards that drove through the wall of the livery and pierced a telegraph pole. Chickens, their feathers stripped from their bleeding bodies, hurtled through the storm, living missiles of destruction that splattered against walls and burst holes through the few remaining windows of the general mercantile.

Then, with greater suddenness than its appearance, the tornado raced onward across the prairie, its deadly tail lifted now and the incredible sound of its passage abated. In the stillness, Charlie Wilks croaked.

"Go get Bob and the kids."

Evan Cramer and the young, runty outlaw returned in a few minutes, bringing along a boy of eight or so and a girl of eleven.

"I told that fat old wife of yours to keep in the cellar with the rest of the kids or we'd paint your house red with their blood," he told the frightened banker.

"Now, *Mister* Hollister, open that safe or we'll blow your kids' brains out," Charlie Winks threatened.

"You wouldn't dare."

The shot sounded enormous in the confines of the brick bank. Brains, blood, hair and bone chips flew from the side of the boy's head.

"Jamie!" the horrified banker screamed.

Evan Cramer quickly opened the fly of his linsey-woolsey trousers and exposed his engorged organ. "Now, get to work on that safe, banker, or I'm gonna shove this into your daughter there, then shoot her like Bob did yer boy."

"No, oh please no. I'll do as you say. Spare her please."

Hollister's hands quaked as he reached for the combination dial.

"That was a shot," Rebecca said as they entered the shattered town of Tribune.

"From the bank," Lone Wolf added.

"I knew I saw some of Tulley's men here yesterday. What a perfect time to rob the bank."

Only a few dazed victims of the tornado wandered aimlessly on the streets, surveying the damage, oblivious to the heavy rain that still fell. Rebecca and Lone Wolf trotted their horses in the direction of the bank. From the other direction, the marshal came on the run.

"There was a shot fired from the bank, Marshal," Rebecca told him.

He looked at her blankly, not recognizing her with her hair in braids and wearing her squaw dress. "Looks like you two are the only ones weren't knocked silly by the twister."

"We saw it hit and came to offer help."

"First let's take care of whoever is in the bank." Woody Steinert turned toward the brick building and cupped one hand at his mouth.

"You in the bank. Come out with your hands up."

"No chance, lawdog!" Evan Crammer taunted back. He punctuated his words with two shots from his Colt.

A wind-borne sheet of rain obscured the front of the bank. The marshal fired back and missed.

"We got the banker and his little girl in here, Marshal. Back off or we'll kill 'em both."

CHAPTER 4

Two citizens appeared half way down the block. One carried a Sharps buffalo rifle, the other a shotgun.

"We heard shootin', Marshal," the nearer one called out.

"Got some hardcases in the bank with Mr. Hollister," the lawman told them.

"Then let's get 'em out," the second volunteer suggested.

"Not that easy. They say they'll kill Hollister and his daughter if we don't pull back."

Rebecca and Lone Wolf held a brief conversation. "Marshal, I think we might be able to help. It's risky, but better than taking a chance with their lives."

Suddenly the peace officer recognized her. "Say, you're the lady was in my shop yesterday askin' about a wagon train."

"That's right. And unless I'm entirely mistaken, those men in the bank are from the Bitter Creek Jake Tulley gang."

"Never heard of them until you mentioned the name yesterday. Ain't wanted in Kansas."

"They are now," Rebecca countered. "Bank robbing is a crime, isn't it?"

"Hummm. What's this idea of yours?"

"You start talking to them. Try to make a deal for them to release the banker and his girl. While you do that, Lo . . . er, my partner and I will slip around back. We should be able to get a shot at them through a window."

"You? You're gonna take them on in a shootout?"

"There isn't time to explain everything, Marshal. So far I have personally killed eleven of Tulley's men. I can handle a revolver and a rifle well enough to make it count. Do you agree to this?"

"Well, like you said, it is risky . . ."

"Marshal," Cramer's voice interrupted. "Get those people off the street or the kid dies."

"We're going," Woody called back. "You don't want to hurt that girl. Now, let's talk about this." He gave a significant nod to Rebecca.

The marshal and two townies backed across the street, while the barber-lawman continued to talk to the outlaws. Rebecca and Lone Wolf walked away, out of sight at the corner. They hurried quickly along the side street to an alleyway. Debris from the storm choked the entranceway. They climbed over it and moved with practiced stealth through the sodden leaves, crumpled cartons and shattered spears of wood. Lone Wolf had his bow. Rebecca had her Smith and Wesson .38 ready in her right hand, a gleam of anticipation in her eyes.

"That should be the back of the bank," Rebecca whispered close to Lone Wolf's ear. "Watch the glass."

Gingerly they stepped over the scattered shards, careful not to grate any of them against the porous soil underneath. A voice came to them faintly from inside, through the empty sash.

"I'm working as fast as I can," Hollister protested. "only two more numbers."

"Make it quick," an unknown man growled.

"Marshal," a familiar voice called out. "We can talk as long as you like. Thing is, us boys ride out of here free as air, or we blow holes in two of your citizens. Which'll it be?"

Neither Rebecca nor Lone Wolf could hear Woody Steinert's reply.

"Go to hell, Marshal. This is gonna be done our way . . . or else."

"There, it's open," the banker announced.

"Now," Rebecca whispered with a nod of her head. She stepped into the opening created by the storm and took aim with her Baby Russian.

A flat report sounded inside the bank and fat Charlie Wilks pitched forward with a small hole at the base of his skull.

"What th' . . ." Bob Tolle blurted. He turned toward the window in time to catch Lone Wolf's arrow in his chest. The feathered shaft ripped through his right lung and came to rest with the fletchings touching the front of his rubberized slicker. The sharp metal pointed protruded from his back. He feebly tried to raise his Colt. Rebecca shot him between the eyes for good measure.

Evan Cramer spun away from the front of the bank. "Charlie . . . Bob! What's happened?" He gazed uncomprehendingly at their bodies, then started to raise his revolver and shoot the quailing Hollister girl.

Rebecca's next bullet smashed the ball joint of his right shoulder at almost the same second Lone Wolf's

37

arrow plunged deep into the opposite one. Evan Cramer let out a groan of anguish and sank to his knees.

"Don't shoot me. I give up."

"Go tell the marshal," Rebecca requested of Lone Wolf. "I'll keep him covered."

Three minutes later, the wounded bandit stood in the middle of the street, in custody of Marshal Steinert. Angry folks gathered around, muttering.

"Go get the judge," Woody Steinert ordered one spectator. The man hurried off amid words of approval from the rest of the townsfolk.

"We'll hold his trial right now," the lawman explained to Rebecca and Lone Wolf. "No sense in stringing it out. We can use the Rooster Tail saloon. It don't look too badly damaged."

The rain had slackened, though not entirely stopped. Everyone stood about sopping, hair bedraggled and hanging in wet strings down the sides of their heads. Steinert, with Rebecca and Lone Wolf at his sides, frog-marched the prisoner to the saloon. On the way, Lone Wolf sent a prayer of gratitude to the Great Spirit that he had been wise enough to change to the white man's linen bowstring. Although it still sounded odd at the release, compared to the gut string he had used for nearly ten years with the Crow, it had the advantage of functioning reliably in any sort of weather.

A man in a black frock coat and trousers entered a few minutes later. He carried a large, leather-bound book tucked under one arm and a cartridge-studded gunbelt looped over the other, the ivory butt of a Colt Peacemaker protruded from the holster. The bardog put a chair on the mahogany and the short, rotund man in formal clothes climbed up to it. The barman handed him a bung starter and sat an empty beer barrel beside the seated man.

"Court will come to order," the judge announced in a testy voice, as he rapped the wooden mallet on the top of the barrel.

"Before there's any trial, your honor, I would like to question the prisoner," Rebecca requested.

"A woman, no less. That's an unusual request. Why do you wish to interrogate him?"

"I'm certain he has information I badly need. It's about a gang of outlaws he ran with, or still might be connected to."

"Hummm. I . . . see. Go ahead, young woman."

"I'd rather talk to him alone. With the marshal there, of course."

"Take him in the boss's office," the bartender offered.

"Yes," the judge agreed. "That will do."

Once alone with Cramer, Rebecca got right to the point. "You rode for Jake Tulley at Grub Stake, right?"

"What's that to you," the surly robber growled.

"I was there. I killed a lot of your friends. Now I want some answers, or I'll kill you."

Cramer's eyes widened. "You *are* Zeke's niece. Well, I'll be damned."

"Very likely. How soon depends on how well you cooperate. Where is Jake Tulley now?"

"I don't know."

"That's a lie." Rebecca reached out and grasped the shaft of Lone Wolf's arrow. She looked directly into Cramer's eyes and coolly began to twist the slender length of wood.

Cramer screamed. Woody Steinert, who leaned against one wall whistled tunelessly to himself and pretended to ignore the entire scene.

"Where is Jake Tulley?"

"Stop. Stop it, will you? He . . . he's somewhere east of us. Most likely in Indian Territory by now."

"With the wagon train?"

"I've said all I'm gonna."

"No, you haven't." Rebecca calmly shoved another half-inch of the arrow into his tormented muscle.

"Stop-stop-stop!" Cramer begged. "I don't know all about that set-up."

"Tell me what you do know."

"They're stealin' young white girls. All blondes."

"What for?"

"I don't . . ." Cramer's denial ended in a shriek when Rebecca tapped the nocking slot of the arrow with the barrel of her Smith and Wesson. It drove the point nearly through the outlaw's arm.

"What for?"

"Tulley an' Roger Styles have some sort of deal set up. They're sellin' the girls to some feller down south somewhere. Honest, that's all I know about it. It's good for a lot of money, though. I heard that."

"Who was with you on the bank robbery?"

"Bob Tolle an' Charlie Wilks. Bob was on his way to join Tulley an' we had him string along. Charlie was with us in Colorado."

"I know. Where were you going from here?"

"To meet up with Tulley." Cramer talked freely now. Fear of more pain loosened his grasp on his tongue. "He's supposed to cut through Indian Territory and the corner of Arkansas, then the wagons go on due south."

"To where?"

"I honest don't know."

Rebecca made a motion toward the arrow again.

"I mean it!" Cramer shouted.

"That all?" the marshal inquired.

"I suppose so," Rebecca acknowledged.

"Better have the Doc patch him up before the trial. He might not last through, after what all's happened."

"Whatever you say, Marshal," Rebecca agreed, stepping away from the pain-wracked prisoner.

Twenty minutes later the trial began.

"This court is now in session, the honorable Karl Bielefeldt, Justice of the Peace presiding. Has a prosecutor and defense counsel been selected?"

"No your honor," Marshal Steinhert informed the judge.

"All right. We'll get to that. I suppose you can do the prosecutin', Linc."

Linc Thompson, the general mercantile owner stepped forward. "Ain't got my Sunday clothes on, Judge."

"We'll overlook that formality. Now, how about someone to defend this murderin' scum? How about you, Frank Meyer?"

A shabbily dressed individual in stained bib overalls shuffled forward. The dull glint in his eyes spoke of limited intelligence. *"Ja,* sure. I can do it, too. I'll get you free, feller. Bet ya a biljun."

"Now then, we need a jury. You twelve fellers there by the faro layout. You'll do fine. Just mosey over here by the bar." He turned to Linc Thompson. "Are you ready for the prosecution?"

"Yes, your honor," Linc Thompson intoned solemnly. "I have no opening statement, because I don't know for sure what went on. I'll call as my first witness, Milton Hollister."

The banker had gone home, disconsolate in grief over the murder of his son, but when Marshal Steinert sent for him, he came to see justice done. He stepped up before the bar and raised his hand to be sworn.

"Now, then, Milt, tell us what happened."

Hollister related his story, including the brutal slaying of his eight year old son. Tears ran down his face as he told it. Many of the women among the spectators crowded into the saloon openly wept with him.

"Then the man who actually pulled the trigger is dead?"

"Yes. Killed by that young woman over there."

"Oh's" and "Awh's" went around the room and all of the townspeople turned to get a look at Rebecca Caldwell. Thompson turned back to the banker.

"That's all. Will the young lady in question please come forward, give her name and be sworn."

Rebecca stepped up to where Hollister had stood and, in imitation of him, raised her right hand. After the oath, she faced Linc Thompson.

"Now, then, Miss Caldwell. Is it correct that you shot the actual murderer?"

"I didn't know who was who at the time. But I shot the one called Bob after my friend, Bret Baylor put an arrow in him."

"An . . . arrow?"

"Yes. He fancies the bow."

"What was the defendant doing at the time?"

"Threatening to kill the banker, Mr. Hollister, and his daughter if they weren't allowed to leave the bank with their loot."

"I see. Any questions from the defense?"

"Nope," Frank Meyer managed.

"The prosecution rests, your honor."

"Are you ready for the defense, Frank?"

"You betchum. Now, Judge, you folks on the jury. This man is an outlaw, a thief and a killer. He's done a lot of bad things in his life. *Ja,* sure. The worst, I guess was to be a part of this robbery an' murder. You can look at him and see he's sorry for what he did. All I can say on his part is that I guess whatever is done to him, he deserves. That's all, Judge."

"Aren't . . . aren't you going to ask me any questions? Haven't you got something else to say?" Evan Cramer bleated. His face had gone pasty white and his hands trembled violently.

"What good would that do?" Frank Meyer inquired. "You was caught red-handed."

"Gentlemen of the jury, you have heard the testimony given and now you have time to consider your verdict."

"No! Wait! I got a right to say something," Cramer yelled, coming to his feet.

"Sit down and shut up or I'll have the marshal clonk you one with his six-shooter," Judge Bielefeldt snapped. "Now, as I was sayin', you have an opportunity to consider your verdict. The evidence is clear and the law is exact on this matter. Anyone involved in a murder is as guilty of the killing as the one who did it. That's all."

The twelve men lined along the bar muttered for several seconds. "Your honor, we don't need to go somewhere and talk this over."

Bielefeldt seemed surprised. "You mean you've reached a verdict?

"Yes, we have."

"What is it?"

"Guilty."

"Then you should consider some recommendation of sentence."

"We already have."

"And what is that?"

"Hang the bastard."

A murmur of approval rippled through the spectators. A man at the front of the room stepped out on the porch, then returned, his voice high with excitement.

"The rain's stopped, we can hang him now."

The crowd cheered.

"Nooo!" Cramer wailed.

"Take him out there," the judge ordered. "Linc, get a good length of hemp from your store. Charge it to the town."

"You bet, your honor."

The residents of Tribune, ignoring their damaged homes and the recent storm swarmed into the streets of the battered town. At the far end of the main drag a tall, thick-limbed old cottonwood stood, as it had for centuries. A smoking scar ran along one side, where lightning had struck, and not for the first time. One particular limb had a smoothly worn place on the bark. Its cause became apparent to Rebecca and Lone Wolf five minutes later when a buckboard was wheeled into position under the spot and Linc Thompson arrived with a sturdy coil of manila hemp, one end tied into a hangman's noose. Several onlookers applauded.

Reason had deserted Evan Cramer. He jibbered and spittle ran from one corner of his mouth. It took three men to bring the slack-limbed outlaw to the buckboard and stand him on it. Two others pulled out the tailgate and long iron bolt that supported it. The marshal tossed the noose over the limb and gave it a tug. It had a nice spring in it.

Cramer howled like a banshee as the loop of rope was fitted over his head and the thirteen twists of the knot tightened down. Rebecca and Lone Wolf stood at the edge of the crowd. Beside the young woman an over-dressed dowager glared hotly at the marshal and judge.

"Evan Cramer, you have been found guilty of murder in the first degree. It is the decision of the jury that you deserve death for this offense. As presiding judge I now pronounce sentence on you. You shall be immediately hanged by the neck until dead. And may the Almighty have mercy on your soul. Do you have any last words?"

"Jake? Jake, help me! *Help me, Jake!* They're gonna kill me!" Suddenly his mood changed and he glowered at the assembled townsfolk. "You'll regret this. You'll wish you did as I told you. Jake Tulley'll come here and kill every man, woman and child. So help me, Go . . ." His words cut off when the marshal signaled the wagon's owner and a whip crack put the team into motion, the wagon box leaped out from under Evan Cramer's feet.

His body plummeted down and stopped abruptly a foot short of the ground. The bones of his neck broke audibly and the twitching corpse voided its bowels and bladder while it twisted and swayed on the tightly stretched rope.

The crowd cheered.

"That's simply barbaric," the over-weight dowager muttered to Rebecca. "It violates all the prisoner's rights. He should have been given time for an appeal."

"What need was there for an appeal? He was caught in the act, his confederates killed. The gang they ran with is far more barbaric than a hanging," Rebecca answered her back. "They've looted and murdered in more places than you can count. Besides, the way I see it, an appeal would be a waste of time since it is only a means for the guilty to avoid punishment while the innocent suffer."

"Wherever did you get such outlandish ideas, girl?" the dedicated do-gooder demanded of Rebecca. "Why . . . why, that undermines the very cornerstone of American justice."

"Not really. That . . ." she pointed to the dangling cadaver, "is the way American justice should work. The guilty pay and the innocent are avenged. There isn't any such appeal process, as you are talking about, in Oglala justice."

"Ogla . . . whaaa . . . You're . . . you're an Indian!" the woman reacted excitedly, examining Rebecca's clothing and hair style for the first time, her mouth twisted into a moue of distaste.

"No, Ma'am. Only half," Rebecca reassured her. "That way, you see, I'll only take half of your scalp lock." She grinned wickedly.

Eyes wide, the plump matron uttered a little squeak of distress and hoisted her skirts. With bustle quivering, she shuffled hurriedly away down the street.

"Let's ride out of here," Rebecca suggested to Lone Wolf. "Somehow, that old sow spoiled my day."

CHAPTER 5

"At first, I couldn't believe it." The speaker, although severely wounded, sat upright against the wheel of his buckboard and puffed on a pipe. A man in his mid-thirties, he had lived through an experience that added the necessary strength to relate his tale.

"They looked like Injuns. Rode right up and started shootin'. I got hit early on, fell off the wagon. My brother an' his wife, they didn't fare so well. Both killed and their daughter taken off by those renegade whites."

Rebecca Caldwell knelt beside the man, offering him small sips from a canteen. A frown creased her smooth, high forehead. "They took the girl?"

"Yep. Seems that's all they was after, too."

"How long ago?"

"Can't tell you, rightly. Day or two ago. I come around long enough to patch up this hole in me, then blacked out for a while. We were headed for Coldwater. It's a wonder the horses haven't died. Me, too, for that matter."

"You're certain they were whites, dressed as Indians?"

"No doubt in my mind. They was talkin' in English once they thought us all dead but the girl."

"Which direction did they go?" Rebecca inquired.

"Southeast, toward Indian Territory."

"We're ten miles south of Coldwater," Lone Wolf remarked as he returned from a near-by creek where he had watered the wagon's team. "Can you make it from here?"

"Me? Oh, sure. If that bullet didn't do for me an' a couple of days without any grub can't put me away, I can ride a wagon all right. I, ah . . ." a slightly puzzled expression crossed his face when he looked back at Rebecca. She appeared to be a white girl, about eighteen or so. Yet her beaded doeskin dress and the Indian garb of her companion could mean they were part of the gang that had attacked him and his brother. Then he dismissed that idea. After all, they had stopped to help him. If they were with the renegades, they would have just shot him and rode on. "I gather you're on the trail of these owlhoots. I don't mean to be rude, but, ah . . . What's a, ah, woman doin' a thing like that for?"

"To get even for five miserable years that they're responsible for," Rebecca told him in a hard, flat tone. "Was your niece blonde?"

"Yep. Prettiest yeller hair and big blue eyes."

"What is her name?"

"Ruth Ann."

"When we catch up to the men who did it, we'll see she is returned to you."

"That's mighty nice. I appreciate that. M'name's Coaker. John Coaker. Got a little place on the Salt Fork River. Get my mail in Hardner. You can reach me there any time."

"We'll get your Ruth Ann back, I promise you,"

Rebecca said vehemently. "And all the other girls."

"Others?"

"Yes. Enough to make killing their captors a pleasure."

"I'll not do it. Never, never, never," Amy Branson exclaimed defiantly. She hurled the slim book of etchings across the wagon box and folded her arms across her young chest.

"You have to look at the pictures," Lisa informed her. "Miss Hattie will pinch you good if you don't."

The big Conestogas rolled over a rough trail through the red rock country of Indian Territory, headed nearly due eastward toward the Arkansas border. Amy had continued to chafe at her captivity and urged other girls to plan a means of escape. She frequently received vicious pinches from the horse-faced woman who supervised the girls. Her throat felt raw from the clouds of russet dust that rose from the little-used road they traveled. Even so, she defended her position.

"Those things are nasty. They show people doing awful things."

"They're not awful," Lisa countered. "It's like what my sister, Sally, did with cousin Roddy. We've got to learn those things to please the men we're being sent to. Miss Hattie says."

"Miss Hattie is an evil old woman who wants to hurt us. I hate her," Amy fired back. "I hate her so much I want to take a knife and . . ."

"Don't!" Lisa cried. "You'll get us all in trouble,

Amy Branson. I don't want to sit here and listen to you."

She rose and stuck her blonde head through the opening in the canvas top to speak to the driver.

"I want to go to the wagon ahead," she announced sweetly.

"That's all right with me," the rough-voiced man replied. He slowed the team and Lisa clambered off the big conestoga.

She didn't go to the next wagon, though. Instead, she ran far to the front. "Miss Hattie, Amy Branson is at it again. She says she won't look at the pictures. Said she wanted to take a knife to you."

"You're being a good girl to tell me this, Lisa. Come to see me tonight after supper and I'll give you a special treat for it."

"Like the last time?" Lisa asked, eyes glowing. "I like that."

"Of course, dear. We get along just fine, you and I. Now, I'll go take care of that willful brat, Amy."

As the sun lingeringly set over the Osage Hills country, Bitter Creek Jake Tulley and Roger Styles sat around a small fire removed from the main part of the wagon train encampment. They sipped from tin mugs of Roger's prize brandy.

"Captain Decker will meet us when we get off the boat," Roger informed his partner in crime. "It's a good thing we sent him our route of travel. That letter I got in town today is important."

"Yeah. Why does he want us to get to New Orleans ahead of the wagons?" Tulley queried.

"He's nervous is all," Styles depreiated. "This is a

risky business. One slip and we'd all see the inside of a prison."

"But it pays well. Even better from what you told me."

"Yes. Those fat old potentates in Arabia are all rich and they sure hanker for young girls. From what Decker related to me one time in Denver, some of 'em can't even get it up unless they've got a real young, blonde girl."

Tulley snorted derisively. "For what I hear, some of 'em as figger a pretty little boy just as good."

Roger ignored the remark. "We'll have to arrange to leave the train in Hattie's hands before too long, so we can reach New Orleans in time. Figure out who you want to take with us and who should stay to watch the wagons."

Not realizing it at the time, Rebecca and Lone Wolf and the five Cheyenne Dog Soldiers pursued a false trail. It took them much further south than the wagon train had journeyed. On their third day after crossing into Indian Territory, one of the younger Cheyenne warriors, who had been scouting ahead, returned to the main body with exciting news.

"Kiowa village ahead," he announced.

Immediately, the Cheyenne, traditional enemies of the Kiowa began to prepare for war, producing paints and looking to their weapons.

"There will be no fight," the scout told them, smiling. "It is a large encampment and they are preparing for the sun dance."

"How do you know this?" Sure Knife questioned.

"I rode close enough to see. Their lodges are many and are arranged in hoops of circles around a wide empty space in the center. A stake was driven into the center of this empty ground. It was dressed like a scarecrow. The Kiowa call it a *T'au*. While I watched a race was held and warriors counted *coup* on the *T'au*, just like a man."

"If we interrupted their ceremonies," Rebecca suggested, "surely they would kill us."

"No," the young brave informed her. "I have been among the Kiowa as a small boy. This thing I know. They are forbidden any war-like act or even to quarrel in the time before and during the sun dance. There are some white men nearby, with many of the stinking meat animals. The Kiowa don't like that and the whites don't trust the Kiowa, but the Kiowa do nothing about it. We can ride into the camp and be welcomed, for that is the custom of the sun dance."

Rebecca decided at once. "Then that's what we shall do."

Hundreds of Kiowa greeted their arrival. Children ran laughing and shouting and dogs barked wildly. The sponsor of the sun dance, a venerable chief named Broken Drum, made them welcome. Lodges were found to accommodate the guests. A few warriors eyed the Cheyenne braves suspiciously and fingered the hilts of knives or hafts of tomahawks in their sashes though not a hostile word was spoken. Then Broken Drun called for a council with the pipe bearer of the Cheyenne.

After they had smoked and spoken together, the old, white haired chief summoned Lone Wolf and Rebecca and a Kiowa brave named Spotted Rump.

The pipe went its rounds, the three Indians obviously a bit uncomfortable with a woman at the council fire. At last, Broken Drum rose and addressed Rebecca, though he looked at Lone Wolf as he spoke.

"We are gathered here for the sun dance. Yet, in this happy time, the Kiowa are troubled. White men and their cattle, the stinking meat, are not far from here. Their presence disturbs the spirits. It also disturbs me," he added wryly. "We have sent messengers to them, requesting that they go away. This had been refused. The long horned animals must be rested and allowed to graze a few days before going on. We can not force them to go. Nor can we move the location of the ritual. It has been selected by prayer and vision. If the cow, ah, herders . . ."

"Cowboys," Rebecca supplied in English.

"If the cowboys come as peaceful guests to the sun dance, it is possible they might not understand our ways and trouble could result. This person of the Red Paint People," he pointed politely with his chin to Sure Knife, "tells us that you have great medicine and are known as White Robe Girl among your own people, the Sioux." Broken Drum used the "cut-throat" sign language symbol to clarify the Kiowa word for the Sioux.

"*Hecitu welo,*" Rebecca acknowledged in Lakota. To her surprise, it was the young Kiowa, Spotted Rump who translated her words.

"That is true," the youthful brave spoke in Kiowa.

"Since you are also part white, will you talk with cowboys and work out some sort of solution?"

Rebecca considered for a moment. "Let me think on this. I am not sure how much good I can do, though I will try on behalf of such generous hosts as the Kiowa."

"That is good," Broken Drum grunted. A smile illuminated his seamed face and lent a twinkle to his deep-set, black eyes. "Now let us eat and talk of pleasant things."

After the feasting, as they walked through the sun dance camp, Lone Wolf inquired of Rebecca, "What do you think you can do?"

"I haven't the first idea," she replied candidly.

Toward evening, when all the feverish activity of preparing the camp for the celebration had ended, the soldier orders formed a parade. They had painted themselves and their horses with heraldic designs that identified them in battle and were, among the Kiowa, hereditary. They wore all their best ornaments; hairpipe breast plates, silver gorgets, strings of beads tied to their scalp locks, earrings and pendants. Each man entitled to do so wore his war bonnet and all carried shields and personal weapons. Red marks were painted on their spirited chargers to represent wounds they had received. The procession would be led by the most noted war chiefs.

Here and there among the waiting participants, two men could be seen mounted on a single horse. This, Spotted Rump explained to Rebecca and Lone Wolf before he departed to join his own contingent, was to commemorate an episode in which one man had rescued another from the face of the enemy or borne him away after his own pony had been killed in battle. A few moments later, the parade began.

Each society, in order of its rank, cantered in single file around the inside of the camp circle. In the lead came *Ko-eet-senko*, followed by the others, the Rabbits—boys from seven to thirteen—bringing up the rear. Once the grand inner circle had been completed, they rode out on the opposite side of the sun dance lodge space and circled the outside of camp. When the parade ended, the warriors unsaddled their horses and went to their lodges to enjoy the meals prepared by their women. Rebecca had been given a place in Spotted Rump's lodge.

Traditionally, the men dined first, then the boys, followed by women and girls. Spotted Rump explained to Rebecca that the next ten days would be given to singing, dancing, horse racing and buffalo chases. Such entertainments, he speculated darkly, might be spoiled by the presence of the cowboys and their herd of longhorn cattle. In the evenings, the warrior societies would engage in singing and dancing contests. Almost immediately, he excused himself to join his own soldier clan, the Black Leggings. If any member was late, or failed to attend these contests, he would receive no mercy from his brothers the next day, Spotted Rump explained. The hazing would be terrible. It left Rebecca alone to contemplate the problem of peaceful settlement between the cattlemen and the Kiowa.

CHAPTER 6

"Of course it will work," Amy Branson whispered to the two girls beside her. "Everyone is asleep, aren't they? We crawl over the tailgate and tiptoe out of camp. Stay in the shadows. We put on our shoes once we get away. Flora an' me have gone barefoot more than we've worn shoes," she informed the third youngster. "So you step where we do and it will be all right. Now, let's get started."

They crawled from under the covers, fully dressed. Following Amy's plan, they had waited until the lantern had been extinguished in their wagon, then redressed. Lisa had gone off in a pout earlier and they anticipated no trouble. Stealthily, Amy led the way over the rear partition of the wagon and dropped silently on bare toes to the gravelly soil of western Arkansas. She motioned to the remaining pair and they soon joined her. After they glided off into the shadows thrown by a stand of large, wide boled trees, Lisa Jones detached herself from the darkness at the side of the Conestoga and hurried to Hattie Ketridge's wagon.

"They're doin' it tonight," Lisa breathlessly informed the woman. "Amy an' Flora an' Millie. Sneakin' out barefoot the way we came in here."

Hattie ran blunt fingers along Lisa's jawline. "How precious of you to let me know, my sweet Lisa. We'll put a quick stop to that." She roused herself and one of her large, firm breasts peeked out through the opening of her silk dressing gown. Lisa stared at it with an expression of mixed envy and excitement. One hand went to her own bony chest, finger and thumb gently kneading the nipple of a budding breast, and she thrilled to the sensations it released in her as it hardened.

Outside, in the warm summer night air, Hattie went to where some of the guards slept under their blanket rolls. "Pete, Lou, Red we got some runners. Three of the girls headed out on our backtrail. Split up and go bring 'em back."

"Yes'um, Miss Hattie," Pete agreed.

"You and I'll head along their tracks, while Pete an' the others slip off to the sides," Hattie told Lisa.

Together, the woman and girl hurried into the night. Less than five minutes later, they heard a cry from ahead.

"Ow! Let go of me," Amy protested.

"Quit wigglin' around, you little bitch or I'll smack you a good one," Pete growled.

"Don't hit her," Hattie purred as she glided forward out of the darkness. A cloud blew away from the moon, revealing the captured girls, firmly held by the three burly outlaws. Two of them sobbed while Amy glared defiance at the men and Hattie. "We don't want them marked up badly when we get to where we're going. I'll take care of that one."

Hattie reached out and caught a thick fold of Amy's left cheek. She pinched it with ruthless force as she drew the girl to her. "You are going to stop being trouble, my little chicken, or you'll never see your twelfth birthday. Your foolishness has gotten all three of you in trouble." She delivered harsh pinches to each of the girls and then herded them back toward the wagons, aided by occasional painful kicks to their small posteriors. They all received another round of nips and a switching with a willow branch before being sent to their beds.

"From now on, I'm going to make sure you stay put," Hattie informed them. She produced a trio of single manacles, which she snapped on their wrists and secured the free end of chain to bolts in the sides of the wagon.

Before breakfast the next morning, the girls were released. "Lisa told on us," Amy said with surety. "We aren't gonna let her get away with it, are we?"

"But what can we do?" Flora asked, eyes wide with fright.

"I have a plan."

"It had better work more than your other one," Millie cautioned.

"It will. In the medicine box on the chuckwagon I saw a bottle of *Pluto Water*. Do you know what that is?"

"N-no," Millie responded. Flora shook her head.

"It's what you take when you can't go. Only a little bit and it loosens you up like a cow eatin' green oats," Amy explained. "Let's be real nice to Lisa for a while. I'll steal the *Pluto Water* and we'll mix up a drink with some rosewater and sugar. She'll never know until it's too late."

The rebellious trio giggled over the prospect.

Late that afternoon, after much sweet talk and playacting on the part of Amy and her friends, Lisa forced the wagon train to make an early stop. Somehow, she had come down with a violent case of diarrhea.

Rebecca and Lone Wolf, wearing white man's clothes rode into the trail camp of the Texas cowboys. After the howdies had been said, the white squaw got down to business.

"We've been in the Kiowa camp. They're making ready for a sun dance. That's big medicine for them. They feel it would be better for everyone concerned if you took your cows a bit further up the trail."

The foreman, a big, raw-boned, sun-browned man with trails engraved in his leathery face, rubbed his chin and shook his head from side to side. "Lady, I don't know how you got mixed up in this, but it's more'n it appears."

"Please, call me Rebecca and I'll call you Archie."

"All right, Rebecca. Like I was tellin' ya, this is a bit complicated. I got a thousand head of longhorns I'm pushin' up to the railhead at Abilene. We've been on the trail for dang near a month and a half. These critters are gettin' skinny. There's prime grass here. Up a ways, that ain't necessarily so. We got to feed 'em some or they'll never make it. In Kansas those damn sod-busters charge rent on their unused grassland, so it figgers this is the best place to do it. We got no argument with them Injuns, but we got as much right to graze here as they do to hold their silly dance."

"The Kiowa don't quite see it that way. They agree, they have no quarrel with you. But they want you to reconsider moving somewhat further north."

"Cain't do it."

"Would you . . . be open to a proposition?"

"What's that?"

"A small wager. You know how Indians like horse races. Outside of personal bets, there'd be an agreement that the winner would stay on and the loser move away from this area. What do you say to that?"

The idea had come to her early that morning. Two days had passed without any inspiration, then, while watching preparations for one of the many horse races the Kiowa held as part of the preliminary festivities to the sun dance, she had realized what avid gamblers they were and recalled similar contests among the Oglala. Could cowboys, who spent much of their lives in the saddle be very different in this respect?

A glint appeared in Archie Powell's eye. "Well, now, I'd have to take that up with the boys," he evaded.

"Winner gets to keep both horses."

Greed overweighed caution. "I think I can persuade them. When would this race be?"

"This afternoon."

"I'll send word after our noonin'."

"That will be fine."

Rebecca returned to the Kiowa and presented her idea. Whoops and shouts of excitement told her of the general approval of her plan. Quickly the camp police set about driving stakes into the ground to mark the course. A good mile and a half, when they finished, the layout ran a snake's back route through and around the tableland where the Kiowa encampment stood. It crossed the creek at one point, rounded two large cottonwoods and ended where it started.

Two short minutes after one o'clock, a pair of cowhands rode into the camp. They asked to see Rebecca and when the girl stood before them, with Broken Drum at her side, the spokesman addressed her with his hat in hand.

"I reckon we got us a horserace," he told her. "What time will it be and where?"

"Right here, say an hour from now?"

"The boss'll go for that."

Every member of the Kiowa band turned out. The betting started heavy and stayed that way. All but the herd guards came from the trail crew. They brought with them a short, skinny kid of fourteen, introduced as Junior Lattimer, and a broad-chested, leggy horse of a sort Rebecca had never seen before. The riders, Lattimer and Spotted Rump, were walked over the course and heard the rules explained.

No lashing a rider with a quirt, no hand holds and no clashing of horses, simple regulations, but enough to please both sides. The jockeys swung into their saddles.

"Ready . . . Get set . . . GO!" Lone Wolf called out. He fired his revolver at the sound of the last word.

At the start, the big chestnut under Junior Lattimer bounded ahead by half a length. Spotted Rump slashed his quirt at the flanks of his fastest pony and tried to close the distance. The two horses pounded over the red soil, past a throng of cheering, warwhooping spectators, and on toward the first turn. As they came out of the turn, Lattimer had increased his lead to three-quarters of a length. Shouts of approval rose from the cowboys.

Both riders disappeared into a low draw and only their dust told of any progress. Junior Lattimer held in the big stallion the best he could, though the powerful runner had lengthened the distance between them and Spotted Rump by a bit over a full length by the time they splashed into a creek and headed for the next turn.

Spotted Rump, a compulsive gambler, had bet nearly everything he owned on this race. So far all he had seen ahead of him was a big pale-brown rump and flying blond tail. As he thundered across the prairie toward the big cottonwood where they would ride around and start off on the third leg of the race, he flailed at his mount, urging more speed, bent far forward, streamlining his push through the air.

By the time they reached the tree, the Kiowa had closed up much of Junior's lead. In desperation now, Spotted Rump let his pony out all the way. He edged up to half a length, then only a head difference. So confident of victory, the young brave and Chief Broken Drum had never considered the possibility that they might be forced to cancel the sun dance because of having to move from the appointed spot. Such a thing would not happen.

Then Junior let the stallion out a little.

The gap widened to a length, then a length and a half. In the distance the last tree swelled in size as they hurtled toward it. Two lengths separated the racers when Junior swung close in around the cottonwood and pointed his mount's nose toward the finish. Both sides cheered frantically at their booming approach.

Maintaining his two length lead, Junior Lattimer flashed past the finish line and halted the big steed in a shower of red dust. He felt wildly elated. What a sweet-running horse!

Spotted Rump was humiliated, also destitute. How could he have lost? Rebecca came to him and noted the scowl on his forehead.

"The best horse won," she told him simply in Lakota.

"Were they fairly matched?" he asked back in the same tongue.

"That's what we were told. A cowpony against your best." Then she added as an afterthought, "Though he looked awfully good for a common cowpony."

"I have lost everything but my loincloth."

"If you'd lost that," Rebecca teased him, "every girl in camp would be chasing you."

"Even you, *Sinaskawin?*"

Rebecca appraised the lean, muscular body and the sturdy thighs that must shield a truly remarkable lance. She felt her desire begin to burn. "Even me, Spotted Rump."

"Be careful," he cautioned playfully. "You, I might let catch me."

With a light laugh, Rebecca walked away. She happened past Archie Powell and some of his hands, when one of them spoke up in a braying tone.

"That was sure some idea you had, Archie, puttin' up the boss's prize racing stud against that scrawny Injun pony. Shee-it! Weren't no contest at all. I made me some nice profit in pelts and bead work, too."

A racehorse, Rebecca thought angrily. Quickly she sought out Broken Drum. A thunderous rage darkened the old chief's face when he learned of the deception, but he gave no outward sign. He only grunted and dismissed the woman. Spotted Rump soon learned of it.

"This is sun dance and there can be no killing," he told two of his closest friends. "That doesn't mean we can not steal this prize horse. Let us wait until it is night, then sneak up on the white men's camp and take this fast horse from them."

"Yes. Yes," the companions agreed.

"Where's that galdanged stud horse?" Archie Powell demanded angrily when he rode into the Kiowa camp shortly after dawn the next morning. "I know some of you bucks done took him. He belongs to our boss, Mr. Sutter. He'll have our hides," he went on to Rebecca who stood looking at him with the same impassivity as the Kiowa.

"He was gettin' a big fee for that swift racehorse o' his to breed some mares in Kansas."

"You shouldn't have run him in as a cowpony, Archie," Rebecca replied sweetly.

"Are you behind this?" Archie snarled. "Women mixin' in with man's doin's is always a bad thing. Where's that there Lancelot?"

"I haven't any idea. But if I may make a suggestion, I think it wise if you let my friend, Bret, here and I go looking. You don't want an Indian uprising on your hands, do you?"

"I . . . why, I . . ." Archie cooled down quickly at the thought of this possibility. "All right. I'll give you until sundown, two days from now to produce that horse." He wheeled his mount and galloped angrily out of the camp.

"Now we have a horse to find," Lone Wolf muttered under his breath.

"Yes. And I haven't seen Spotted Rump. He never returned after the singing last night."

"You think he . . ."

"Who else?"

After a hasty breakfast, Rebecca and Lone Wolf set out. They made wide, spiraling passes through the prairie until they encountered the tracks left by Spotted Rump and his friends.

"They won't have gone far," Rebecca commented. "Not with the sun dance going on."

"Besides, the way Spotted Rump sees it, his hiding out a day or so without being caught makes the horse his. He'd ride back into camp on that racehorse and think nothing of it."

Two hours later, they found the three Kiowa. They had picketed their ponies and the stallion and were swimming and playing in the creek like small boys. Rebecca explained a plan she had worked out during the hunt and Spotted Rump agreed to give it a try.

"What do you mean, another race?" Archie Powell growled.

"That's what I said. This time, a fair one. Your pick of any good cowpony against Spotted Rump's choice from his ponies. He hasn't given them all away to cover his bets yet. This time he thinks he will win. It's that, or you'll never see that stallion again."

Archie glowered at Rebecca when she finished. "Meddlin' wimmin," he muttered like a curse.

"In an hour, then?"

In this race, things would be a bit fairer, Rebecca had decided. It would be for a quarter mile. A cowpony against a buffalo pony—noted for its quick starts and short bursts of stamina. The riders would be the same.

"I don't like the looks of that shaggy brute," Archie grumbled to a couple of his wranglers when they arrived for the race. "Could be they're pullin' a fast one on *us,* this time."

At the signal, Junior Lattimer and Spotted Rump mounted up. Archie Powell made the start.

For the first hundred yards, the two horses remained neck and neck. Then the sturdy, rangy buffalo pony inched ahead by a nose. Then a head. Dust flew from the pounding hoofs. Spotted Rump yowled at his pony like he did in a buffalo chase. The valiant, though cantankerous, creature responded with all its strength. Coming down to the quarter mile pole, the Indian mount had its opponent by three-quarters of a length. The Kiowas went wild. Glumly, the cowboys had visions of their bets flying away, like the hoofs of the shaggy-coated beast.

Then Junior Lattimer urged a final burst of speed from his favorite lineback and the two riders crossed the finish line nose and nose. A dead heat.

"Tie, by damn!" Archie shouted above the excited yells of the spectators. "All bets off."

Broken Drum came forward, holding the reins of

the big stallion. "Here your chief's horse," he said in broken English.

"I'm mighty relieved to see him again, Chief," Archie allowed. "To . . . to show there's no hard feelin's, I'm gonna cut out a couple of nice steers and we'll have us a barbecue, Texas style. You like that?"

"Tex-as style good. Take many horses, scalps, much blankets in Tex-as," the chief replied through a smile.

"Ah . . . that's not exactly what I had in mind, Chief. But you'll see. We'll do it up big. And some dancin' an' fiddle music afterward. Maybe a few drinks of whiskey between us chiefs, eh?"

"Whis-key good. We feast, drink, dance all night."

An hour before sundown, Spotted Rump rode through the camp, a long stemmed pipe in one hand. He called out as he slowly walked around the rings of lodges. "I am Spotted Rump. I have led five raids in moons gone by. I have taken up the pipe once again. When the sun dance ends, I join the Oglala warrior woman, *Sinaskawin*, in her search for the evil whites. Who rides with Spotted Rump?"

Although anxious to get on their way, Rebecca knew it would be unforgivable rudeness to leave before the final ceremony of the sun dance. Archie Powell and his cowhands, badly hungover, with several grinning, secret, happy smiles as the result of friendly invitations from Kiowa women, drove their herd an additional ten miles north of the camp and exchanged further presents with Broken Drum.

At last, three days later, the center pole was cut down amid all proper ritual, skinned and carried to its place of honor in the wide space at the center of camp. Once erected, a young medicine man climbed to the fork at the top where he prayed to the sun for some ten minutes while everyone present stood at attention. The buffalo robe taken from the designated kill in the ritual hunt two days before was produced and fastened over a framework bundle of cottonwood and willow to resemble a living buffalo. This was lashed to the fork by the man atop the center pole, then he slid to the ground.

Quickly materials were gathered and the lodge constructed. After the day-long ceremony, in which Rebecca and Lone Wolf did not participate, Spotted Rump came to them. "Two hands and one of warriors have smoked the pipe with me. We ride with you with the coming of tomorrow's sun. Take many scalps. Have much fun."

Rebecca thought of the Tulley gang and the depredations they had committed in the past. She had five Cheyenne and a dozen Kiowa ready to kill for her. For Tulley, such a fate did not seem at all out of line. She smiled at the earnest young Kiowa.

"Yes. I am sure you will have lots of chances for that."

CHAPTER 7

The thunderstorm blew up out of the southern portion of Indian Territory. Fierce, lashing winds tore at the small mounted party as they struggled along a ridge, the other side of which was in the state of Arkansas. Hail, the size of bullets for the 45-70-500 drove them to find shelter under an overhang. Crowded together, animals and people, Rebecca still had to shout to be heard above the fury of the storm as tons of rain fell in thick, white sheets, drops the diameter of a ten dollar gold piece.

"We should have known the wagons hadn't gone so far south," she told Lone Wolf. "That's cost us two more days. They are moving slowly, but I hate to let more time go by."

"Nothing to do for it. This storm should slow them more," Lone Wolf offered. "We'll put out scouts the minute the rain lets up."

Lightning, crashing into a tall, thick pine a hundred yards away, strobed their movements in its actinic glare. The tortured wood sizzled and popped and the tingly odor of ozone filled the air. Horses tried to bolt. The clap of thunder that accompanied the powerful bolt came immediately, shaking the ground and threatening to deafen them all. Several of the

Kiowa rolled their eyes, round and white with awe for the forces of nature. Blackness had replaced the sunlight of mid-day. The fat, stygian bellies of rank upon rank of thunderclouds stretched to the southwest. Howling gusts blew chill rain in on them until everyone became soaked.

Wind in the twisting, creaking trees moaned like the damned souls of hell and nearly continuous explosions of celestial violence drove out even the ability to think. Rivulets of water formed, widened and became gushing streams that eroded away the edges of the overhang that protected them.

"We have to get out," Lone Wolf yelled to Rebecca.

"In this?"

"Look. The embankment is giving way."

A quick examination told her Lone Wolf had been right. "We must leave," she told Sure Knife and Spotted Rump. "The ground will fall in on us."

"The sky spirits are angry," the Kiowa warrior countered. "We will be smashed out there."

"Better than being buried alive," Rebecca retorted.

The sodden party had not made fifty yards along their route before, with a muted roar, a large section of the dirt outcrop collapsed. Spotted Rump looked with growing appreciation on the wisdom of this strange warrior woman who led them.

For fifteen blinding minutes, in which it became necessary to walk and lead the animals, they struggled against the tempest. Inches of rain fell over the hour they had sheltered at the overhang. More inches cascaded out of the tumultuous sky as they forced their way upward. At the crest, dimly perceived in the distance through the on-going cloudburst, the lowlands on the Arkansas side had turned into a swamp. Young, green cattails and tall wisps of reeds showed above the dimpled surface of a large, trapped body of water.

"If those wagons are down there, they're in trouble."

"So are the little girls they have stolen," Rebecca said in response to Lone Wolf. She looked to her right and, through the closely spaced white streaks of the downpour, saw a dark, nearly circular opening in the hillside. She pointed to it. "Over there. It looks like a cave."

"We'll head that way," Lone Wolf yelled back.

Another ten minutes of slipping and sliding in the mud and sodden leaves brought the hunters to the security of a large, airy cave. Flint and steel quickly produced a fire from dry buffalo chips carefully protected for this purpose in Spotted Rump's parfleche bag. In a short while later, a stew of dried onions, peppers and buffalo meat bubbled over the glowing droppings.

"When the storm ends, we have to move on," Rebecca told the warriors. "We will eat, rest and feed the horses here. No more stops until we locate the wagons."

Long shadows fell over the dirt streets of Fayetteville, Arkansas and women's voices could be heard calling to the children who splashed barefoot through the mud puddles, their shrill shouts of joyful abandon tingling the air. Rebecca Caldwell and Lone Wolf, wearing their "civilized" clothes, walked their horses down the main street as the large, pretentious clock in front of the bank rumbled and tolled the hour of three o'clock, in imitation of Big Ben. The rain had ceased during the night and, because of the numerous washouts and flooded areas, it had taken most of the next day to progress the few miles from the cave into town. For obvious reasons, the seventeen warriors had remained out of sight in a copse of trees in order not to create a stir among the populace.

Half a dozen idlers had gathered around a man standing in front of the livery, his mud-spattered mount drinking deeply from the wooden water trough, while he related the latest gossip to his audience. As the vengeance-bound pair rode closer, his words could be clearly made out.

"Ain't never seen the like. Bunch of stubborn fools, bent on their own destruction, I'd call it."

"Where'd you say they was, Sam?" a spindly loafer with thinning hair and a receding chin asked.

" 'Bout twelve mile east o' here, Chet. Headed *east* if ya can imagine it. Seven wagons, all mired down in the mud and ever'body workin' like ants to free the wheels. I hallooed them from a distance and dang if they didn't show iron and run me off. Like I say, touchy and mule stubborn. *Dumb,* I allow. Nobody in that much need of help turns away an offer."

"Were there a lot of, ah, children on that caravan?" Rebecca asked over the heads of the others. Ike snorted at the heady scent of other horses and rippled his hide, one small, sleek ear cocked toward the sound of a mare in heat inside the stable.

"Sure were, Ma'am. Whole passel of little bitty

girls, as I recollect. Funny, I don't remember seein' a single boy-kid."

"Awh, come on, Sam," Chet argued. "A string of wagons headed east and most of 'em children? What you been drinkin'?"

"Ain't had a snort in two days," Sam protested. "I'm tellin' ya what I seen an' that's the truth. Crazy, the whole lot of 'em. Runned me off when all I wanted to do was offer to bring help."

"How badly are they stuck?" Rebecca queried again.

"Without help, they won't be movin' from there for two, three days."

The white squaw and her companion exchanged thoughtful glances. They turned their horses away from the small knot of people and rode on down the street. Ike snorted his regret at being taken away from the obviously willing mare and grunted in protest when Rebecca thumped her heels into his flanks to urge him to a canter.

"We shoulda let that feller bring some help," Lou grumbled to Pete as they struggled to wrestle a high wagon wheel from the gummy mud.

"You crazy? Anybody get a look at all these little girls and we'd have a hell of a time explainin' it. Push now."

The cargo of captive children had been herded together under a tall elm tree, guarded by three alert hardcases who eyed some of the older girls lustfully. Hattie Ketridge stood nearby, watching with impatient vigilance. Beside her, Lisa sucked on a hard candy and slowly, sensuously rubbed a hand along the inside of one thigh, enjoying the tingling feeling it sent through her young, slender body. She eyed her particular enemies, Amy and Flora, and silently plotted their downfall.

Her current plan revolved around a box of rat poison she had found in the supply wagon. Somehow, if she could get them to eat enough in their food . . . When the cook had discovered his *Pluto Water* missing, the cause of her discomfort had become clear. Only it could not be proven, even to Miss Hattie's satisfaction, that Amy Branson had been responsible. There had to be a way to make them pay. Waiting for the wagons to be pulled out of the mud was boring. Lisa turned away and rubbed higher up her thigh, taking comfort in the warmth it spread outward from her loins. In the distance she heard the thud of hoofs and wondered who it might be.

"Hello the wagons!" a woman's voice called a few minutes later.

Rebecca and Lone Wolf halted some fifty yards from where a dozen men labored to free the mired Conestogas from the slippery mud of Arkansas. At last she saw the cause of new grief among the Oglala so far north of here. The stranded vehicles didn't look all that menacing. The armed men did, though.

"Y'all ride on. We don't need no help," a lanky man with stringy yellow hair called out in reply to their hail. He cradled a Winchester repeater in his left arm.

"We . . . we're the ones looking for help," Rebecca

invented. "We got caught in that storm yesterday. Our pack mule ran off and we're without food or blankets. We're lost, too. Can you help us?"

"There's a town about ten, fifteen miles back the way you came," the armed guard responded. "Best bet, you go there."

"But, we're hungry," Rebecca appealed, making use of her helpless expression.

The lean man consulted a stocky, hard-faced woman who had walked down a small hill to his side.

"Best give them some grub, Sam," Hattie advised. "It's that or kill 'em both. If we turn them away, they're likely to do a lot of talking."

He turned back to Rebecca. "If you can make use of some beans, flour and bacon, we can spare a little," he offered.

"That would be nice. We'll ride in and get it."

"Naw. I'll bring it out to you."

Five minutes later, laden with a large burlap bag of supplies, the guard approached Rebecca and Lone Wolf. He handed the sack to the tall, muscular man astride an Indian pony and stepped back. "Y'all best be movin' on now, hear?"

"Thank you for the supplies," Rebecca said sweetly. "Only . . . why are you all so stand-offish?"

"Important cargo. Orders from our boss not to let anyone get close. Sorry, but you know what that means."

"Surely," Lone Wolf put in. "We thank you again."

They rode off, carefully storing their images of the train, its strength in armed men and the nature of their weapons.

* * *

An hour later they met with their Indian allies. Lone Wolf gave a detailed description of the strength of the bogged down wagons. After he concluded, everyone sat a while in thoughtful silence.

Spotted Rump rose at last and spoke slowly. "They are strong. But they cannot move and we outnumber them. We should attack and kill these people. We number three hands and four. Most have guns. It would be easy."

"Yes," Rebecca agreed. "Only what about the captive girls? Some of them could be killed. Or Tulley's men might finish them all off to get rid of witnesses against what they had done."

"We came to fight," Spotted Rump countered.

"We must be clever to win and not have the girls killed," Lone Wolf put in, supporting Rebecca.

Sure Knife stood. "The way to do it is sit off at a distance, hidden in the trees and shoot the men one at a time."

"They have horses. They could make a run for it. And, again, they might kill the girls," Rebecca protested.

Silence returned for a while. During the wordless contemplation, excitement built in Rebecca as she considered the words of the two pipe bearers. A plan, incomplete, but workable, began to form. At last she suggested her strategy to the others.

"Spotted Rump is right. We must attack the wagons. Sure Knife is also correct in saying our best advantage lies with sniping at the outlaws. Here is a way we can do both and not endanger the girls." She paused, collecting the rest of her stray thoughts. "The four best shots can conceal themselves in the woods near the wagons. They will shoot at specific targets. Lone Wolf and I will ride separate from all of you. When the rest attack openly, we will come to the 'rescue' of the defenders. After that, they should show some gratitude to us. We will plan the raid for late in the day. If we are lucky, we will be asked to stay the night. Once inside their camp, we can manage to help the rest of you slip in. After that, it will be too late for the guards to do anything."

Carefully she laid out the plan of attack from within the circle of wagons.

CHAPTER 8

All but two wagons had been freed from the gluey mud and formed into a tight circle by an hour before sundown. Hattie Ketridge fumed at the risk involved in spending yet a third night in the same place. Forced to stop by the rain, then mired by clinging gumbo, every hour increased the risk of discovery by those curious enough to cause trouble. The consequences of intervention by the law remained on her conscience as she supervised the preparations for the evening meal.

Not a thought entered her mind, though, of the type interruption that did occur.

Two of the sentries posted for the night grunted, spun sideways and fell to the ground a fraction of a second before the sound of shots rolled across the glade where the kidnappers had pitched camp. Instantly the air filled with shrill war whoops and pounding hoofs and a force of painted savages came sweeping down on the startled whites.

"B'God, Injuns!" Sam yelled at Lou.

"Where'n hell did they come from?"

"Shoot now an' ask questions later," Sam advised. "Else we won't be around to ask."

The attackers split and began to circle the wagons in traditional plains style. Hattie studied their tactics while she ducked bullets and fired at the hooting warriors. Damn, what were they doing here? The ones painted in red must be Cheyenne. But this far east? Something was wrong with all of this, yet she couldn't put it straight in her mind. Another of the gunslicks provided by Jake Tulley screamed and went down with an arrow in his chest. Hattie stopped trying to figure it out.

With a swirl, the braves broke off and withdrew a short distance, then raced back. Tulley's startled men had recovered their senses now and when they fired, two of the Kiowa braves flipped off their ponies. One of the Cheyenne grasped a badly wounded arm, though he continued the charge. Shots came from the far side of the desperate camp and voices shouting in English.

"Come on, men," Lone Wolf's baritone bellow declared. "We got 'em now." He fired his Winchester '68 with all the speed he could employ. Beside him, Rebecca blazed away with the pair of Smith and Wesson Americans she carried as horse pistols, a gift from Matt Peterson in Grub Stake. The Indian attack wavered, then broke off. The warriors streamed away on individual courses, not to be seen again.

Still dressed in their white man's clothing, Rebecca and Lone Wolf galloped directly into the camp, firing in the direction of the departing savages. Hattie recognized them as the pair they had provided supplies to earlier in the day. She stepped forward, a heavy Spencer carbine in her hands.

"I must say we're glad to see you get here," she began. Then her eyes narrowed with suspicion. "Where's the posse you were leadin' back here?"

"No posse," Rebecca answered her. "We heard the shooting and came to see what had happened. We thought if the Indians believed there were a lot of us, they'd be scared off. Looks like it worked."

Hattie's hard features remained rigid with troubled doubt for a while longer, then softened slightly and the bray she used as a laugh came from deep inside her. "By damned if it didn't," she cawed. "You done right well, there, Miss."

"Thank you. My name is Rebecca . . . Clark and this is my friend, Bret." Rebecca paused and looked around. "With, ah, those savages out there, could we, ah, appeal to you to let us stay here the night?"

Hattie gave them a hard appraisal. It could end in trouble, she considered. But then, they had provided the distraction that broke off the attack. To turn them out would seem even more suspicious. She forced a cracked smile.

"Sure, dearie. Least we can do for you after the risk you took to help us. Make yourself at home."

After a supper of corned beef, boiled potatoes and cabbage, Rebecca and Lone Wolf began to spy out the location of sentries and the general condition of the defense. As she worked her way behind a screen of brush that afforded a bit of privacy for the latrine trench, Rebecca was approached by a small, blonde girl who motioned to her shyly.

She followed the girl a bit farther from camp, then spoke quietly to her. "What is it? Why did you want to talk to me?"

"We . . . we're prisoners of that awful woman. It's true, believe me," Amy Branson began in a rush. "My name is Amy Branson. There are twenty-three of us and we're being taken somewhere to be . . . to be sold to men."

"I know, Amy," Rebecca said reassuringly.

Amy blanched. "T-then . . . you're . . . you're one of them?"

"No. We're here to help. Now tell me the rest."

"We are all treated bad, pinched by Miss Hattie if we don't do as she says. She also stuck her fingers in . . . ah, in here," she indicated her pubic region. "It was to see if we were still, ah . . . you know."

"Still virgin." A scowl had darkened Rebecca's fair features and her deep blue eyes had darkened to nearly black.

"One of the girls, she was twelve or so, didn't pass the test. One night, she . . . she disappeared. Miss Hattie said she had run away. But . . . I don't think so. And there's Lisa. She's one of us, but she spies on us for Miss Hattie and does her bidding. I hate them both but . . . well, we're all afraid of them. If you came to help us, please, please do something so we can escape and run away. Or get away as fast as you can and go get the law. It won't be long before it's . . . too late."

"Don't worry, Amy. That's exactly why we're here. Before morning, you'll be free."

"Oh, I'm so happy!"

A rustle in the brush stopped their conversation. Lisa Jones appeared, a sneering smile on her lips. "I thought I saw you sneak away, Amy. What are you doing here with this stranger?"

"We only . . ."

"Call of nature," Rebecca smoothly inserted. "You can understand that, can't you?"

"I can tell you two were plotting something awful. You're looking to get punished again, Amy. When you do something bad, everyone suffers."

"Everyone but you," Amy blurted out, her anger rising to overcome worry.

"You shouldn't have said that, Amy," Lisa taunted. She turned suddenly and hurried off in the direction of the wagons.

"Oh, oh, I just know she heard everything we said. She'll go right to Miss Hattie. You'll have to run for your life and then . . . and then we'll never get away."

"Take it easy, Amy. I think I can get her to see reason."

In five fast strides, Rebecca caught up to the small informer. She grabbed Lisa by one shoulder and jerked her around. "I want you to listen close to this. You are going to say nothing about what you saw or heard to anyone on this wagon train. Is that clear?"

"I'll do as I please. Miss Hattie likes me and she won't let anything bad happen to me."

"Not this time. Hear me good, Lisa. When I was fourteen the same men who kidnapped all of you took me to the Sioux. I lived with the Oglala for five years. I learned how to be exactly like them." From its hiding place in the waist of her riding skirt, Rebecca removed her thin-bladed, razor-edged Oglala skinning knife. She let the cold starlight play on the metal while Lisa eyed it with round, frightened eyes. "I am part Sioux, myself, so it was easy. I can skin a deer or a buffalo in no time with this. It will also take the hide off naughty little girls who tattle on their fellow prisoners." She paused and motioned Amy closer.

"Amy, don't let Lisa out of your sight. Watch her close and if she makes any attempt to reach Miss Hattie, come tell me. I'll slit her throat from ear to ear."

Lisa gasped and Amy produced a sickly, but relieved, smile.

Satisfied on that account, Rebecca concealed her knife again and led the girls back into the firelit circle. She went to confer with Lone Wolf. Of particular importance, she had not noted any of Jake Tulley's key men in camp, nor seen any sign of the outlaw leader himself or Roger Styles. That meant that freeing the kidnapped girls was only the beginning of her search.

CHAPTER 9

Even the owls had given up their nocturnal search for food. Their mournful hoots had faded into silence when Rebecca and Lone Wolf rose silently from their bedrolls and slipped stealthily through the camp on moccasined feet. Each had a half-circle of hopefully drowsy sentries to deal with.

Rebecca located her first one leaning his right side against a wagon wheel. She quickly clapped a hand over his mouth while she plunged her knife into the small of his back, hacking back and forth with it to destroy the kidney. Then she stabbed him on the other side. A wave of nausea rose from her stomach when his hot, slick blood washed over her knifehand, though she fought it down and lowered the corpse to the ground. She wiped her fingers clean on his shirt and chucked his weapons into the brush outside camp. Then moved on to the next victim.

Lou yawned prodigiously and stretched to relieve the cramped muscles occasioned by his long hours on watch. He'd be glad when this job had ended. The way some of those little gals went around wiggling their butts, it kept a feller's pecker stiff all the time. At least, he thought with fond recollection, before they had finished her off, he and Sam had got to hump that gal who'd turned out to have already lost her cherry. Good and tight, he remembered, his loins warming, and juicy, too. She'd taken them both on twice and enjoyed it as much as they. Too bad the orders were to kill her. Damn! Old Maw Thumb and her four daughters were a poor substitute. Lou yawned again, his head thrown back to the sky.

The knife in Rebecca's hand slid into the hollow of Lou's throat and slashed veins, arteries and his gullet. He convulsed violently and tried to shrink from the blade, then died with a gurgling sigh. Like the shadow of a night hawk, Rebecca slipped through the sleeping camp.

On the opposite side of the circle, Lone Wolf approached his third, and final, sentry. The man moved from his spot and leaned his Winchester against a stump. Shoulders hunched, he turned outward from the wagons and began to relieve himself. Swiftly, Lone Wolf moved up behind him.

"Huh?" he managed an instant before Lone Wolf's hand closed over his mouth and wrenched his head backward. Cold steel traced a deep line of fire around his throat and a fountain of blood gushed out to spray the brush. The outlaw's legs thrashed and his heels drummed the ground for three long seconds, then he went slack and still. Lone Wolf lowered the corpse and glided off to meet Rebecca.

Rebecca Caldwell wondered if she would ever feel really clean again. She had used a knife on Bobby O'Toole—which had been a well deserved piece of irony—and before that another man had tasted a blade in her hand. Even so, the sickly rich smell of so much blood, and to have such a quantity spill over her hands and wrists, left her a bit queasy. She wiped at the sticky substance between her fingers once again and then stepped away from her final kill. Lone Wolf materialized out of the moonless night and nodded to let her know he had finished his task.

A loon's wistful night call summoned the warriors.

"We outnumber them now," Rebecca told Spotted Rump in a whisper when the Kiowa and Cheyenne crowded around. "Spread out through the wagons. The men are sleeping in blankets. Try to keep it quiet. And remember, the woman is mine."

Half a dozen of Tulley's gunslicks died silently in their blankets before one suffered only a wound. He quickly drew his Colt and blasted open the stillness of the night.

"The Injuns is back!" he yelled. "Ever'body up!"

Two more shots speared orange trails in the dark before Sure Knife smashed the man's skull with a tomahawk. Others, aroused from sleep, got into the fight.

Four more revolvers barked, amid strident shrieks from the frightened girls and a bellow of rage from Hattie Ketridge.

Rebecca saw the dark form of a half-clothed man rush in front of her. The Smith and Wesson .44 in her left hand belched flame and the figure flew to one side, stumbled and went down. She cocked back the hammer again and started toward Hattie's wagon.

Lisa, entirely naked, leaped from the back of the Ketridge wagon. In the flickering yellow-orange light of muzzle blooms, Rebecca noticed absently that the girl's hairless cleft had opened wide in arousal, its color heightened by strenuous manipulation. Lisa screamed in horror at the sight of a towering Cheyenne brave and turned about in confusion, uncertain where to go to seek safety. Amy appeared suddenly and charged the other girl. She wound strong fingers into Lisa's long, blonde hair and jerked her to the ground.

"I . . . I must have fallen asleep," she apologized to Rebecca. "She only just got away from me."

"Looks like she had something else on her mind besides telling Miss Hattie about the escape," Rebecca remarked, glancing down at the nude figure.

Likewise unclothed, Hattie Ketridge stood in the open bow at the back of her wagon, her Spencer carbine in both hands. She saw Amy and threw the butt to her shoulder.

"You bitch!" the woman raged. "You brought this on."

Before she could fire, Rebecca triggered the Smith American. The .44 roared and a fat slug slammed into Hattie's naked hip. The impact flung her backward and the barrel of the Spencer climbed toward the night sky. It discharged and before she could reload, Rebecca ran to her. From up close, to Hattie's eyes, the muzzle of Rebecca's .44 looked like a huge, black cavern.

Her fingers relaxed and the white squaw took the carbine from her. Rebecca showed the weapon to Amy. "Do you know how to use this?"

"Oh, yes. Poppa taught me last year."

"Lever another round in and keep both of them covered, don't forget to cock the hammer."

Rebecca found Lone Wolf, Sure Knife and two Kiowa braves crouched low behind the protection of the chuckwagon. Four of the outlaws had forted up in a high-sided Conestoga and kept the four men pinned down with frequent fire.

"We got some little girls in here," a desperate voice called. "We'll kill 'em if you don't back off."

"Keep firing once in a while to hold their attention," Rebecca suggested while she rummaged in a sidebox until she located a coal oil lantern that had been used earlier. With it, she slipped away into the dark, circling the cluster of wagons.

Unmindful of her surroundings, Rebecca hurried toward where she could employ her stratagem. No one, she reasoned, liked fire enough to willingly be burned to death.

"That's far enough, girlie," a gruff voice spoke to her. A darker silhouette rose against the starry night sky. It was Pete, the man Tulley had left in charge of these hardcases. "The way I see it, you're my ticket out of here."

Rebecca gauged the distance between them. Maybe, she thought hurriedly, just maybe she had a chance.

"Oh, ah, and drop that hoss pistol you got in yer hand."

The .44 American hit the ground. Slowly, Rebecca slid her hand toward the voluminous pocket of her riding skirt.

"You think I'm going to take you away from here?" she asked to distract Pete's attention.

"Yep. That's how I see it."

"Well, then, I suppose I have to do as you want." Her hand appeared again, index finger already squeezing the trigger of her Baby Russian.

The .38 quickly spat twice. Two neat holes appeared in Pete's chest, less than an inch apart. Both slugs and a shower of bone chips ruptured the outlaw's heart.

He rocked on his heels, staring stupidly with glazing eyes, then uttered a low moan and dropped to his knees. Vainly he tried to center his Colt on Rebecca's heaving breast, then his arm went slack and he fell face first into the damp Arkansas soil. Rebecca suppressed a slight shudder of relief and hurried on.

On hands and knees, Rebecca crawled to the blind side of the wagon. She unscrewed the cap to the lantern's reservoir and poured coal oil over the muddle of blankets and cut grass under the running gear. Three fast shots sounded from above her. Involuntarily she ducked low, even though she knew they had not been aimed at her. She managed to keep a lucifer match going on the third try and touched it to the kerosene-soaked material.

A feeble blaze rose, then grew. In seconds, dense smoke climbed upward to enter the wagon.

"Fire!" a voice shouted.

"For God's sake, let's get outta here," another answered.

"What about the girls?" the third badman demanded.

"Fuck the girls," the first man snapped. "I don't wanna die in here."

"Then what about those Injuns out there?" the final member of the quartet inquired.

"They can't get us all, but those flames surer'n hell will."

They tumbled out, two from each end. Rebecca

shot one of them, while Lone Wolf and Sure Knife accounted for the rest. Quickly she jerked the burning blankets from under the wagon and doused the flames with ladles of water from the barrel strapped to the Conestoga's side.

"It's all right, girls," she called to the nearly hysterical children inside. "You are safe. Come on out if you want."

In another three minutes the fight ended. Four men, three of them wounded, and Hattie had surrendered. The warriors herded the prisoners together at the rear of the Ketridge wagon. Slowly, timidly, the girls began to gather.

"There's that dirty Lisa," one muttered. "I want to pull out her hair by the roots."

"Tattle-tale, tattle-tale," two other moppets chanted.

The situation took on the elements of a kiddie lynch mob. Rebecca stepped between the justifiably angry girls and Lisa, who had covered herself and sat sobbing beside Hattie.

"If there is punishment due to Lisa, she will get it. You are all free now. You might think about that instead and how lucky you are." She turned her attention to the disarmed and defeated outlaws.

"Where is Jake Tulley?"

No one spoke up.

"Maybe you don't know who I am. I'm Rebecca Caldwell, Ezekial's niece."

"Th-the one who busted up Jake's gang in the Dakotas and Colorado?"

"That's right," she told a freckle-faced, red-haired gunman. "The one who lived with the Sioux. I learned a lot of interesting ways to make people talk in Iron Calf's camp. Do you want me to use them on you?"

A nervous mutter went among the four hardcases. "N-no. Don't suppose there's any call for that," the red-haired allowed. "Jake and Mister Styles took more'n half the boys and rode ahead."

"When did they leave?"

"Before the big rain."

"Shut up, you blabber mouth," a burly man to his left growled. "Jake'll fix your ass for that."

Rebecca raised the muzzle of her .44 American slightly and coolly shot the belligerent outlaw in the kneecap. He shrieked in pain and writhed on the ground. "You were saying," she prompted the pale-faced man she had been questioning.

"They left before the rains. I don't know where to. Something, though, about the Mississippi River. Honest, Miss Caldwell, they didn't fill us in on anything."

"Why is it that every time one of you scum that ride for Jake Tulley uses the word, 'honest,' I want to laugh? Wherever they went, you had to go to meet them, didn't you?"

"No. Not like that at all, Ma'am. We was to turn south when we hit the Harrison Road, then skirt Little Rock and keep goin' due south. Figure maybe we'd wind up in New Orleans if we went fur enough."

"There was a boat to be waitin' for us when we reached Vicksburg," Hattie Ketridge said weakly from behind Rebecca.

"Where was it to take you?"

"I don't know. My guess, though, would be same's his, New Orleans."

"What for?"

"Why, to sell these pretty little girls to some big shot Roger Styles had contact with."

"Anyone have something else to add?"

Silence greeted Rebecca's inquiry. "Well enough, then. Spotted Rump, have your men guard these prisoners while they harness two wagons. We'll take them back to the law in Fayetteville and arrange to have the girls sent to their homes," she went on to Lone Wolf.

Since the conversation had been, of necessity in Lakota, the outlaws and their former prisoners had no idea of its meaning. The young warrior, his scalping knife wet with blood and three fresh scalplocks hanging from his sash, translated into Kiowa and the work quickly commenced.

"Lord above," the sheriff exclaimed in Fayetteville when Rebecca and Lone Wolf brought in the prisoners. "That's a story to top all I've ever run into. Why, even the marshals comin' through from Judge Parker's court in Fort Smith don't have yarns to match that. All those little girls bein' stole by these lowlifes, eh? What you figger to do with them now that they're free?"

"Somehow they will have to be sent home," Rebecca said simply.

"There's no reason you can't escort 'em, is there?"

"Yes, Sheriff. My friend and I are going on after Jake Tulley and the rest of his gang."

"Well, now. That's hardly the sort of a thing for a young woman to be doing, is it?" the gray-haired lawman sputtered.

Fire flickered in Rebecca's eyes and Oglala war drums throbbed in her voice. "I've been on their trail for nearly a year now, Sheriff. I'm still in one piece and there's a lot of them dead or behind bars. I can handle it nicely."

"Uh . . . ah, I'm sure you, ah, can, Miss Caldwell. Only . . ."

"I'm a woman, is that it?"

"Now, that's not exactly . . . yes. Yes it is. Judging from the brigands you brought here and what you tell me about this Tulley, those men are dangerous. Damned dangerous, if you'll pardon the language. There are lawmen and courts to take care of their kind."

"Jake Tulley has been in prison before. So have most of the men who ride with him. If lawmen and courts can deal with their kind, why is it that others, like Bret and I, have to go out and round them up again?" she retorted.

"B-but that's . . . that's taking the law into your own hands!" the distraught lawman stammered.

"It's also called self-preservation. Or have 'civilized' lawmen and the courts taken that basic right away from us even this close to the frontier?" Rebecca's angry words stung the sheriff. He lowered his eyes and swallowed with considerable difficulty before answering her.

"I . . . I'm afraid you're right, Miss. 'Civilized people don't carry firearms.' That's what they say back East."

"Back East, Sheriff, people like Jake Tulley and Roger Styles are elected to public office by those 'civilized' people so they can do their stealing without resorting to violence. Out here we hang them. Further west, or up on the edge of Dakota Territory where I come from, we kill 'em outright. Somehow, of the three, I prefer our way. We'll be going now, Sheriff. Take good care of the prisoners until the hangman arrives."

"Don't forget your reward money. There were wanted flyers on two of those you brought in and probably more on some of the dead ones. I'll make you out a voucher and you can take it to the bank."

"Thank you, Sheriff."

Outside of town, with a fat stack of gold double-eagles in her saddlebags, Rebecca and Lone Wolf met with the *to-yop-ke* Spotted Rump and Sure Knife, the Cheyenne pipe bearer. She expressed her desire to hurry after Tulley.

"We have taken the pipe to fight this person. So far only one small battle," Sure Knife replied. "I say we ride on."

"That is so," Spotted Rump agreed. "You have proven yourself as a war leader, *Sinaskawin*. If you wish to carry my *to-yop-ke* pipe on the war path against Tul-ley, it is yours. I will follow a warrior woman like you gladly."

Rebecca flushed slightly. "That is very kind and generous of both of you. Remember, though, that each day takes us further from your homes. We are in strange country, with many whites around. You must be careful not to be seen by those who would not understand." The two warrior chiefs said nothing, only stood with folded arms and unreadable faces. "Well, then, we ride now. The sooner we catch up to Tulley, the better."

CHAPTER 10

Although in strange country, with the need to stay out of sight, Rebecca set a good pace. In three days they had nearly traversed the state of Arkansas. Late on the second day, Kiowa scouts working ahead, cut Tulley's trail. It led generally in the direction of Memphis, which would fit with the outlaw's talk about the Mississippi River. A person could get passage on a steamboat in Memphis to go north or south. A few miles west of the small town of Jonesboro, the scouts hurried back to where the warriors waited with Rebecca in a shady hillside glade. Their news brought instant action.

"Many men ride ahead of us. More of them than our men have bullets. One like you say to look for, with funny round hat, not there. Other, tall, yellow hair, not see either."

"It has to be Tulley's men," Rebecca decided aloud. "Where are they?"

"Sun move two hands in sky," came the answer.

About two and a half hours, Rebecca estimated. "Exactly how many?"

"Four hands and four."

"Finish eating," she told the warriors, "then we

ride. We'll catch them when they least expect anything."

Tom Clutter seethed with unspoken sourness. It galled him to be put on drag every damned day. Eat dust, then snort and hack all night. He unconsciously raised one black gloved hand to his tender, red nose. It had blistered and peeled. Too much damned sun, he growled to himself. He was used to working indoors. His pale, sensitive skin, pasty white under his longsleeve shirt, broad-brimmed hat and gloves, prickled with rash and tingled at the prospect of being exposed to the biting rays of the sun. Why hadn't they ridden on with Jake Tulley?

He snorted at the question and took a sip from the tepid water in his canteen. How he sweated. He had no idea that throwing in with the Bitter Creek Jake crowd would involve so much hassle. Not like his usual jobs. Take that proud bridegroom he gunned down. Yeah. Inside, at night. A good price paid for his work. A powerful cattle broker who had wanted the girl hired him. That had been a good one. Heat radiated from his loins as he recalled the horrified expression on the bride's face. He'd reacted the same at the time. The next he knew, he had her white gown ripped off and pawed her small, firm breasts. His cock swelled and he tore open his trousers. He had plenty of time for some fun, he reasoned. No one could have heard the shot, far out on that small ranch. His pallid flesh glowed golden in the lamplight as the swaying shaft plunged toward the screaming girl's body.

He entered her, all wet and juicy for her husband,

and thrilled to her scream when he pierced her maidenhead. A cherry he'd plucked. All well and good. He made it last a long time. She moaned and begged for mercy while he drove his long shaft in and out, at last increasing his pace until the throes of his completion shook him to his toes. He had taken her twice more. She continued to resist and bled a lot. Afterward he had got to thinking.

That hadn't been part of the bargain. The girl was to have been left alone so that the cattle buyer could console her and eventually win her. Not so easy now. Clutter killed her too. He'd liked that. It added some spice to the rape. He had driven his throbbing cock deep inside of her and then slowly strangled her to death. Her spasms and twitches had given him a special sort of thrill. Recalling it now, his engorged phallus pushed out the front of his whipcord trousers and he groaned with the sweet agony of his remembered ecstasy.

Lone Wolf's arrow took Clutter in the left side of his back. The shaft pierced Tom Clutter's back, heart and lung, burst the tip out the front with force enough to rip open his shirt pocket. Impaled on the point was a sack of Bull Durham.

"Goddamn! It's Injuns!" a voice called from the front of the column of outlaws.

Spotted Rump and nine of his Kiowas charged wildly at the surprised white men. They had little to choose from for defense. To the right a sheer drop-off plummeted three hundred feet to the spike-like tops of young pines. A hill with more dense woods lay on the left. Horses milling in dusty confusion, they drew weapons to answer the savages' fire.

Two of the bandits fell in less than a minute. Spotted Rump raised his war lance and waved it in a wide arc. At once, five of his braves swung wide and hit the exposed left flank. Another hardcase flew from his saddle. Then a Kiowa brave slumped over the neck of his surging pony, clung a moment, before he fell with a scream into the welter of hoofs. Spotted Rump decided to pull back and charge again. Then he heard cries from among the outlaws and smiled to himself.

Lone Wolf and the remaining three Kiowa warriors opened fire on the rear of the column with their rifles. In panic and confusion, the gunslingers closed up, pressed from ahead and behind. Lone Wolf took careful aim at one man who appeared to be rallying them and squeezed off the round.

A .44-40 slug smacked into the man's chest and his mount reared, wheeled on its hind feet then went off balance. Shrieking even louder than the man trapped on its back, it plunged over the ledge and fell to the distant trees below.

Two bandits tried to charge the light force that threatened their rear. A Kiowa put two bullets into one and Lone Wolf finished the other. Their dying bodies thrashed in the dust, blood pooling to form macabre mud. A shout rose from the thick center of the beseiged men and five of them started up the hill.

"Now," Rebecca commanded. She and the five

Cheyenne rode out of the trees and pelted down on the quintet who sought to shelter in the woods. She saw their eyes go round with surprised fright and their mouths sag in strangled cries of desperation. Then she triggered one of her .44 Americans.

Smoke obscured the field for a second. Then she thundered through it in time for Rebecca to see one of the bandits double over with both hands clutched to his gut. Her shot had found its mark. The others tried to separate and seek individual salvation. Rebecca took a shot at one.

It missed and she drummed her heels into Ike's sides. The big stallion leaped forward and closed the distance between her and the escaping Tulley man. At the sound of rushing hoofs, he turned his head, haunted eyes glancing at her over his shoulder. She came in close and laid the front blade sight of the .44 on his forehead.

"No!" he screamed a second before twenty nine grains of black powder exploded and blew his brains across the ground as surely as it blasted him into hell. Rebecca thundered on past, seeking another target.

He rode comfortably in the center of the column of outlaws. Tom Clutter's strangled cry from behind came as a total surprise to Big Dick Dawson. He whipped his narrow head around in time to see the young pink-faced gunman pitch forward and fall to the ground. Dawson pursed his thick, colorless lips in rapid succession. The nervous habit had been with him since childhood. He started to yell something when a shout came from the front, Indians attacking them. How the fuck had they gotten here anyway? he wondered frantically.

Rifles crackled from ahead and behind him and Dawson found himself swinging out of the saddle. He crouched in the trail, quivering with fear.

A petty hoodlum before throwing in with the Tulley gang, terrorizing aged storekeepers and old women was more his meat. Fighting Indians he didn't consider a sane proposition. A whirl of feathered scalplocks and the whoops of half a dozen savages decided him when men began to fall all around. He looked to left and right.

"What are we stayin' here for?" he hollered over the rage of battle. "We'll get pushed off that cliff if we can't get out of here. C'mon, let's start up the hill. There's trees there to hide in."

"Keep your place, goddamnit," one of Tulley's lieutenants growled. He had remained mounted and worked now to rally the men and return effective fire.

Dawson heard the meaty smack of the bullet that hit the outlaw's chest. He jerked backward and his horse reared. It spun on hind legs, then went over balance and fell with a hideous shriek. The wounded gunslick's scream of terror rang with it.

"That does it," Dawson shouted. "Let's go."

Four others followed his lead. This was more like it, Dawson thought.

Then, to his sudden horror, more howling savages came out of the trees toward which they ran for shelter and charged down on them. Incredibly, the one in the lead was a woman. Dawson lost his nerve completely and ran in a panic at right angles to the approaching hostiles.

A powerful, unseen scythe bit into his leg and he sprawled face-first into the grass. Some instinct of survival cautioned him not to cry out and he lay still, faking the terrible deaths he could see coming to men all around him.

All thought of resistance vanished with the appearance of Rebecca and the reserve force. They quickly downed the five men on the hill and struck the flank of the outlaw column like a massive boulder. Men shrieked and leaped up, only to die with a lance in their guts. Others scrabbled backward, unmindful of the precipice, and went over feet first, howling in horror at their sudden weightless condition.

Spotted Rump charged his men down on the survivors once again and that broke the last resistance. Only three outlaws remained alive when the shooting stopped. Immediately the Cheyenne and Kiowa began to cut scalps.

"Nooo!" a voice howled from the hill. Big Dick Dawson struggled furiously and tried to break free of the muscular warrior who knelt to take his hair. The bullet wound in his left leg hampered him. "I'm alive! I'm alive," he wailed.

"Don't kill him," Rebecca commanded. "I want to ask him some questions."

Lame Beaver brought the quailing white man down to the beautiful warrior woman who led them to so much good sport. "Tell me what I want to know or I'll let Lame Beaver here scalp you alive," Rebecca told him calmly.

"Anything, anything," Dawson babbled. His sleek

black hair hung in disarray and he continuously puckered his lips.

"Where did Jake Tulley go?"

"To Memphis. To take a boat to New Orleans."

"What's in New Orleans?"

"The man they're dealing with, I suppose."

"Tell me about the deal?"

"I . . . I don't know everything. But it seems that the little girls we rounded up are to be sold to some Oriental princes, potentates in Arabia and Turkey, places like that. They are supposed to have a hanker for very young, blonde girls for their harems. There's somebody in New Orleans that Mr. Styles and Jake Tulley know who can get the girls out of the country."

"What else do you know about it?"

"Nothing. Nothing, believe me."

"How many of those girls did you personally capture?"

"F-four."

Rebecca smiled bleakly. "Let him go," she instructed Lame Beaver.

"You mean it? Really mean it?" Dawson babbled.

"Yes. Grab your horse and run for it."

Gratitude suffused Dawson's face and tears of relief welled in his eyes. He limped painfully to the nervous horse he had been riding and grabbed at the reins. Rebecca waited until he had swung into the saddle.

Then she calmly raised her .44 American and shot him in the head.

"I have to go on," Rebecca told the gathered warriors at the campfire that night. "That means to

New Orleans. You could not move freely in a big white man's city. All of you have fought well. You have many scalps to take home. Sure Knife, tell your Oglala relatives that they are being avenged. Tell them that the law knows they did not steal the girls. All will be peaceful again. If it were possible, I would like to have you along. This way is better."

"We return to our lodges to sing of our victories. Also to sing of the mighty warrior woman who led us to such rich pickings," Spotted Rump declared. "It will always be in my heart that the woman, *Sinaskawin* of the Oglala has powerful medicine. Walk in the way of the Great Spirit."

Sure Knife nearly blushed. "I feel stronger for having been on the war path with you. All that you say shall be told to the Oglala. In the morning we go toward the sun. You ride to its place of birth. Take . . . take this war pipe with you to mark your good fortune," he ended impulsively, extending the ornately decorated ceremonial pipe to her.

"Oh . . . oh, Sure Knife . . ." Rebecca stammered, uncertain if she would do so womanish a thing as start to cry. She sniffled once, firmly, then kissed the tall Cheyenne brave on the lips.

CHAPTER 11

Jonesboro seemed hardly large enough to carry its name. A wide east-west street, part of the High Road in fact, had become the main business district. Slightly more than a block and a half in length, it did include an office of Harmon and Company, the southern states' stage line. In the mid-morning hours, women in ankle-length dresses of far heavier material than worn on the frontier went about the daily shopping chores. In addition to the ubiquitous general mercantile, Jonesboro boasted a green grocer and two butcher shops. Two residential side streets paralleled Forrest Street—renamed at the onset of Reconstruction for Confederate General Nathan Bedford Forrest. A narrow avenue crossed them, given over to a hotel, boarding houses, two ale houses, a tavern and a pair of tidy inns. Rebecca Caldwell and Lone Wolf reined up in front of the stage stop.

"We'll probably have a wait of a day or two," Lone Wolf told his companion.

"Why is that?" Born and raised on the fringes of the wild Dakota Territory, Rebecca had little experience with the white man's ways.

"There aren't any large towns west of here, so on a

small feeder line like this they won't run a daily coach."

"Let's go in and see," Rebecca suggested practically.

"How-do, y'all," a smiling young man behind the counter greeted them. "Headed West?" He had noticed the cut of their clothing, which although obviously that of white men had a definite western flavor.

"No. To Memphis," Rebecca told him.

The clerk frowned. It wasn't proper for women to take the lead, not . . . civilized. "Two of you?"

"Yes. And we want our horses brought along, also."

"We can manage that, Ma'am. Be an extra two dollars, though."

"Fine."

Tickets were made out and paid for. "When does the stage leave?" Lone Wolf inquired.

"Tomorrow morning, seven-thirty sharp. After you get a room for tonight, you can put your horses up here, save a livery fee."

"That's kind of you," Rebecca offered in gratitude.

"Just a service of Harmon and Company, Ma'am. Our pleasure." Despite his southern upbringing, his eyes glowed when he studied the pleasing curves and promontories of Rebecca's lush young body.

She noted his interest and felt a stirring in her loins. It had been too long. "Do you know of anyone with vacancies? We'll be needing, ah, *two* rooms."

"Over at Fairchilds'. They've plenty of room and good food, too. My people run it. I'm Doug Fairchild."

"Why, thank you, Mr. Fairchild. I'm Rebecca Caldwell and this is Bret Baylor, my, ah, business associate."

"Pleasure, Miss Caldwell. Goin' down river?"

"Yes."

"Cattle?"

"Yes."

Doug Fairchild proved much more talkative at the supper table that evening. So did Rebecca. Their eyes communicated much that their voices did not. They found each other sufficiently young, healthy and magnetically attractive. After the meal, the gentlemen boarders excused themselves for a smoke on the verandah. Rebecca and two spinster school teachers retired to the sitting room for coffee and short breads. Immediately she found herself missing the light witty conversation of Doug Fairchild.

His comments on the Reconstruction government, laced with biting satire had entertained everyone during the substantial meal of ham, roast beef, okra, corn, potatoes and poke salad. So insipid was the conversation of the maiden school mistresses that she actually felt a sense of release and freedom when she excused herself to go to her room.

She had hardly undressed and slid between cool sheets when a soft scratching came at her door. Her heart quickened. Rebecca threw a light wrapper over her shoulders and padded, barefoot, to the portal. She opened it a crack to reveal a grinning Doug Fairchild. He held a dusty bottle and two glasses.

"I, ah, brought a little scuppernong wine. Thought you might enjoy sharing it."

"That sounds lovely," Rebecca enthused. She threw the door wide and invited him in.

Doug swallowed with some difficulty when he observed her trim figure through the thin material of her gown and realized she wore nothing at all underneath. His hand shook slightly when he cleaned the bottle and pulled the cork. He poured two glasses and handed one to Rebecca.

"To your very good health, Miss Caldwell," he toasted.

"Call me Becky, Doug."

They sipped and he refilled. "I . . . ah, you are, uh, a most attractive young woman, Becky."

"Thank you, Doug," she teased. Rebecca decided not to give him an inch.

"I mean, I'm not in the habit of . . . of . . ."

"Romancing every young woman who enters Harmon and Company."

Doug winced. "That makes it sound worse, somehow."

"Then, do, please, say it in your own words." She found she enjoyed the game, Doug's discomfort in particular.

"I . . . well, I find you," he cleared his throat and plunged on. "I find you to be an exception to so many. I'm not a woman chaser. It's only that . . . you'll be gone tomorrow and I wanted to see more of you."

The time had come, she sensed to play the final card. "Would this be seeing enough?" she asked as she slipped the wrapper off her shoulders and let it fall to the floor. Lamplight glowed golden off her smooth, naked body.

Doug nearly strangled on the sip of wine he had taken. "I . . . oh, Becky. You are such a lovely thing. I . . ." Doug ended with a groan of misery as he sensed the hot surge in his loins and the lengthening of his penis.

Her own passion ruled completely now. "Quick. Get out of those clothes. No. Let me help you."

Rebecca stepped close to Doug and began to unbutton his vest, which she slipped off his wide chest. He had gray eyes, she noted, with a mystic, far away cast to them. Neatly parted black hair glowed in the low lamp's rays. Then she began on his shirt. Gently Doug touched her shoulders and a tremble rippled through him at the silken texture. Rebecca slipped his suspenders off and pulled the opened shirt from his waistband. By now, fully engorged, Doug's manhood throbbed with urgency. For some reason, he no longer thought it uncivilized for a woman to take the lead.

He sighed roughly when she started on his trousers. His hands cupped her breasts and he teased her nipples, which rapidly grew erect. When Rebecca exposed his underwear, she gasped at the size of the protrusion. Quickly she pulled the drawstring and slid the knee-length cotton drawers down to his ankles. That left her kneeling with one cheek softly rubbing against the large, blunt tip of his maleness, which peeped from its hood of flesh. She turned her head only slightly and her tongue flicked like a serpent's, to caress the spongy glans.

"Aah! Becky, Becky, no girl has ever done that for me," Doug exclaimed in mounting vigor.

She could hardly contain herself. Her mind filled with all the marvelous pleasures she would obtain that night. Doug's manly lance had a size and firmness that promised not to fail on her and his slender, muscular body, that of a youth in the prime of his endurance, assured her he would not weaken before the sun first poked above the distant line of houses. Slowly she began to take him into her mouth, a moist, warm cavern that sent shivers of delight through his body. He tasted so good! she thought with growing fervor. So sweet and musky. She began to rock on her heels.

Doug trembled and stiffened his back. For a moment, he feared his knees would give way under him. What had he been missing? Becky's tongue cupped to encompass his thickness and he clasped both hands on the back of her head.

"More," he panted. "Take it all."

Gradually, she did. When that mighty snake entered her throat, she began to hum, a quavering tremolo that Oglala women sang while they scraped buffalo hides. It drove Doug wild. His excitement increased hers a hundredfold. She continued her ministrations until he began to pant and utter small cries of ecstasy. Then she withdrew only far enough to allow him space to explode in a cascade of syrupy delight that set off stars in her head and she felt her own completion cramp her belly and send shivers along her spine.

Still staggered by his experience, Doug led Rebecca to the bed. He positioned her on the edge, legs wide spread, her arms behind her back for support. Then he lowered himself until his still rigid member brushed at the lacy folds that guarded her secret portal. With one hand he stroked himself to greater firmness, while slavering his shaft in her freely flowing juices. Then he assaulted her first portal.

It collapsed with tingling eagerness and he plunged on into her depths. Becky's eyes widened with the incredibly superb sensations that sprang from this giant assault on her inner core. She stretched to accommodate and even that brought her greater pleasure. Then their primitive souls merged in tingling, shattering abandon and they sped off to visit the moon and nearer planets.

When the celestial journey ended, they lay together on the sheets, gently touching, exploring each other with shy fingers. Only a few minutes passed before Rebecca's fingers circled his relaxed phallus and began to squeeze and stroke it toward new alertness.

"Again?" Doug inquired in an expectant voice.

"Oh, yes, again. And again, and again."

They parted company in the small hours of morning, an hour before sunrise. Doug apologized that he had to shave and dress to get to work by six. Rebecca lay a long while after he left, body humming with sated delight, remembering how perfect a lover he had been. Too bad, she thought, the stage couldn't be delayed two or three days more.

A group of frowning, uncomfortable looking people waited for the stage when Rebecca and Lone Wolf arrived. Only one, a short, pudgy man with thick, sausage fingers, pink and uncallused, greeted them.

"Howdy-do, folks. I'm Harley Goodall. M'line's ladies unmentionables. Pleasure to see such smiling, friendly faces for our journey ahead." He paused to take a sip from a silver hip flask he produced from an inner coat pocket. "Y'all headed for points east?"

"Yes," Rebecca told him coolly. "Memphis."

"Shoot! Why, that's hardly east at all. I'm on m'way to the big mills up in New England that produce the goods I sell. Then back to the wild Indian country for me. I'm even thinking of expanding my line into Arizona Territory. Lots of folks movin' out that way."

"My, how interesting," Rebecca offered in frigid tones.

A heavy-set dowager standing near by sniffed disdainfully. "Simply shocking," she said to the Reverend Billy Baker. "The Harmons should not allow such conduct on one of their coaches."

"I quite agree, Madam," the preacher intoned in pious notes. "Liquor is the curse of the working class. Far too many men have fallen to the wayside, victims of John Barleycorn." He would have waxed even more sermonic, had not the bulging lady interrupted.

"Quite so, Reverend. My late husband, God rest his soul, occasioned a nip or two, I know it. For all my efforts to the contrary. 'Lips that touch liquor shall never touch mine,' I told him before our wedding. Right then and there he took the pledge, though in days to pass, I frequently caught a scent of whiskey disguised by clove oil on his breath."

"The stage will be about an hour late, folks." Doug Fairchild announced from the doorway to the office. "Bridge washout caused a detour. So you have plenty of time for breakfast at the cafe next door if you missed yours to get here on time. Good morning, Miss Caldwell, Mister Baylor," he greeted. His expression gave away nothing of the intimacy he and Rebecca had shared until an hour ago, though his eyes glowed hotly as their gaze brushed her pert breasts.

As predicted, the stage arrived at eight o'clock. Luggage was quickly manhandled aboard and lead ropes rigged for the two saddle horses. Everyone had barely settled onto the horsehair-stuffed leather seats when the driver cracked his whip and the Concord jolted forward, then clattered off in a steady, vibrating rhythm toward distant Memphis.

Before the coach reached the eastern edge of town, Harley Goodall had swilled twice from his flask. After the second tot, he belched decorously behind his hand.

"Must you," the dowager demanded in a haughty voice. "breathe your obnoxious whiskey fumes on me, my good man?"

Goodall belched again and grinned. "It's that or puff 'em all over the lovely young Miss seated beside me." He inclined his head toward Rebecca.

"Such gall!" the woman exclaimed. "Strong drink is the devil's snare, sir. Kindly desist from bringing Satan into our midst."

"The lady is, ah, right, er, Mr. Goodall," the reverend offered in timid support, despite his greater size than the petticoat merchant.

"Madam . . ." Goodall began sententiously. "What is your name, by the way?"

"Southerby. Mrs. Amanda Southerby of the Vicksburg Southerbys."

"Mrs. Southerby, I have an affliction. Granted it is to John Barleycorn, though that notwithstanding, it torments me with cravings the like of which few people know. I am also troubled by the motion of coaches, rail cars and wagons. A little of the elixir I imbibe which, by the way, consists of honey, lemon juice and the finest Kentucky bourbon, soothes my stomach and prevents its contents from being messily ejected upon the laps of my fellow passengers. Permit me that a few alcohol fumes are of superior quality to that unfortunate circumstance." Goodall belched again and reached for his flask.

A green persimmon could not have produced a more puckered expression on Amanda Southerby's face.

"Many's the man who, in the throes of spirits, invents maladies of the person to excuse his excesses," the Reverend Billy Baker self-righteously intoned toward the ceiling of the coach, as though addressing his remarks to his God.

"You say something, Reverend?" Goodall asked pointedly. "You seem a bit peaked. Perhaps a snort of my medicine would improve your disposition?" He offered the flask, which the good paster shied away from as though a poisonous reptile. "What about you, sir?" the salesman went on, extending the container to Lone Wolf.

"No thanks. Never could countenance lemon juice or honey."

Goodall joined Rebecca in a good laugh.

At noontime, the team was changed while the passengers enjoyed as unusually good meal at the post station. A minute shy of a half hour, the Harmon and Company coach rolled on its way. Thick dust rose from its wheels and Rebecca surmised that the tremendous storm of five days past had not struck here. One hour blended into the next while Mrs. Southerby and the Reverend, heavy with food, napped through the afternoon.

"Any of you folks armed?" Harley Goodall inquired to break the monotonous silence as he reached for his flask.

"Good heavens no," Amanda Southerby replied. "No civilized person carries a firearm, unless riding to the hounds."

Reverend Baker snapped instantly awake. "Firearms? Did someone mention firearms? Filthy things. Tools of the devil. It's not Christian to own a gun you know. *Jesus didn't carry a six-gun.*' That's the topic of a sermon by a colleague of mine, the Reverend Jim Roberts. We see alike on that. It's in the Bible you know, about guns being forbidden to Christians."

Even Amanda Southerby exchanged a startled glance with Harley Goodall at this obviously ridiculous invention. That didn't faze the sermonizing of the good reverend.

"This great nation will never be safe until evil firearms are taken from every Christian hand."

An hour later the coach suddenly jolted to an abrupt halt.

"Stand and deliver," a thickly accented voice demanded from outside.

"Like hell we will!" the lean, lanky shotgun guard roared. His short-barreled Winchester double bellowed in defiance.

Three revolver shots crackled in the air afterward. "Mike!" the driver shouted.

"You want to go the same place he did, driver, just show some spunk."

"We ain't carryin' any valuables," the driver protested.

"Let's have that strongbox from under yer seat," the talkative highwayman demanded. "We know better'n that. You should have some gold in there."

The heavy box rattled, then thudded to the ground. "You done kilt Mike Crouse," the driver complained. "You got the strongbox. Now let us go in peace."

"Not before we empty the pockets of your passengers. Everyone out."

"Oh! Oh, my heavens!" Amanda Southerby dithered. With pudgy fingers she sought to conceal her rings and other jewelry in the bodice of her dress.

"Oh, Lord, protect us from these heathen villains," Rev. Baker prayed, hands clasped and eyes searching for heaven.

"I think *we* could do a better job of that," Lone Wolf muttered.

"I said everybody out! Make it snappy or we shoot holes through the sides."

Amanda Southerby filled the doorway with her fiftyish, vastly overweight body. Stray sausage curls of muddy gray escaped from her bonnet and dangled over her shoulders. Reverend Billy Baker came next. Then Harley Goodall. Lastly, Rebecca and Lone Wolf.

"Okay, folks," came the nasal, New England accent of the leader. "Empty out. Watches, money, jewelry."

"I . . . I have nothing of that sort," Amanda protested.

"Oh? Let's have a look. Ben, check her out," the highway man ordered one of his companions.

"Sure thing, Ned."

Ben swung from his saddle and approached the over-stuffed dowager. His big, grimy hand reached for the bodice of her dress.

"Now see here, young man. This is an outrage," Mrs. Southerby protested.

With a solid yank, Ben ripped open the heavy cloth. A shower of valuables cascaded to the ground. Amanda Southerby wailed in fright and indignation and tried to cover her huge, pendulous breasts that had been exposed in the process.

"What ya yellin' about sister? Nobody's gonna look at them oversized pillows anyway," Ben taunted.

"You . . . you . . . barbarian!" Amanda shrieked.

"Now you, fancy Dan," Ned ordered Rev. Baker.

"I, sir, am a man of gawd. I bear no filthy lucre. Nor the baubles and gadstones of a sinful world. I know of your need and it is greater than ours. In a time of madness it is understandable to be faced with so unsavory a means of providing for wives and children. I sympathize with you, believe me. Gawd will look out for you. Though you have sinned, He shall forgive you and bring you into the fold."

"What's he talkin about, Ned?" another highwayman asked.

"Beats me, Rip." To the preacher he growled. "Stopper that crap-hole and bring out your wallet."

Baker blanched. "It's nothing. Believe me, sirs, only a few small contributions from the faithful for the maintenance of an orphanage. Small children would go hungry without this pittance."

"Pit me no pittances, preacher. Hand it over."

Baker dropped to his knees, hands extended in supplication. "I beg of you. There is only a few dollars here. For the children?"

Ned's Remington cracked and the slug bit into Baker's left shoulder. "We got a saying, us knights of the highway. 'Your money or yer life.' Now hand over."

"I . . . I bet you . . ." Tears ran down the minister's florid cheeks.

Again Ned's revolver barked. This time a red spot appeared, spreading around a puckered black bullet-hole on Baker's right trouser leg. He groaned with great pain and toppled forward in the dirt. Slowly he raised himself on one elbow and reached into his coat. He took out a thickly stuffed wallet and a small leather pouch that clinked musically.

"You'll be damned for a liar, preacher," Ned declared as he received the large sum and thumbed through sheafs of ten and twenty dollar bills and hefted what must be a good three thousand in gold coin. "What did you do? Loot your church's treasury?"

"How dare . . . why . . . I . . . I . . ." Baker's chin sank to his chest in humiliation.

"Be damned," Ben exclaimed. "You hit it right on the head. He's a sneak-thief, all right. You can smell it on him."

"Naw, he only shit his pants," Rip chortled. Two of the bandits, who had remained silent until now joined in the laughter.

"We take risks for what we steal, preacher," Ned told him. "A cowardly thief like you turns my stomach. Collect money in the name of God an' then steal it from folks who trusted you. I think we'll just have to shoot you full of holes for that."

"No. I beg you. Please let me go. I've lost my . . . my stake in life now, I can harm no one. Please!" Baker begged. "It was wrong. I admit that. But so much money at one time. I . . . I . . . couldn't resist."

All the highwaymen turned their eyes on Baker as he sniveled in front of them. Instantly, three hands streaked toward concealed weapons.

Lone Wolf's Remington barked almost in time with Rebecca's Baby Russian. A split second later, a short-barreled .44 roared in Harley Goodall's fist.

Rebecca and Lone Wolf cleaned two bandits out of their saddles. Ben, standing closest lost his right eyeball and a chunk of the back of his head when the two hundred grain slug from Goodall's revolver smacked into him. To the right of the holdup men, the driver made a dive for his dead partner's shotgun. He caught a bullet in the shoulder from Ned for his efforts. By then, the trio on the ground had their six-guns recocked.

Rebecca fired first, cutting a chunk from Ned's left ear. Lone Wolf and the drummer put .44 rounds into

Rip's chest that exploded his lungs. A pink spray whoofed out of his gaping mouth and he went over backward, bounced from his skittering horse's rump and flopped out his life in the Arkansas dust.

Ned managed to send one bullet in Rebecca's direction that singed a raw, reddish purple mark across her left shoulder. It threw her next shot wild though she squeezed the trigger with enough control to put her fourth shot dead center in Ned's breastbone. The little .38 slug didn't finish him, but another .44 from Goodall lifted the highwayman's hat and a large flap of his skull.

"Not bad shooting for an unmentionables drummer," Rebecca complimented Goodall in the quivering silence that followed the shootout.

The hard-drinking salesman blushed slightly. "I . . . I try to keep my hand in. After all, I do work the frontier."

"Where did you get that short-barreled Colt?" Lone Wolf asked.

"Feller I ran into once. Don't rightly recall what town. He had a wagon all rigged up to do gunsmithy out of. Cut off the barrel of my Peacemaker, crowned the muzzle and there you are. Works fine."

Above them, the driver groaned. "I'm startin' to smart some. You folks think you can get your palaverin' over and get on board?"

"We want to load these stickup men on the top, driver," Lone Wolf told him. Already Rebecca had started to climb the big front wheel to tend to the driver's wound. "There might be some reward money on them."

"Should pay for a patchup on my shoulder," the salty teamster snapped. Then he groaned when Rebecca cut away the sleeve of his flannel shirt. "Name's Butler, Leige Butler, Miss. Sure do appreciate this. Ain't often somethin' like this happens."

"I know. 'Civilized persons don't carry firearms.' " Rebecca answered him sweetly.

"I'm mighty glad you folks do."

Voices from down below interrupted the repair job.

"Here, Reverend," Harley Goodall offered. "Let me give you a hand. Those wounds will need tending to."

"Keep your hands off me, you murdering drunkard!" the man of God snarled. He jerked his head to include Lone Wolf. "You, too. You killed those men in cold blood when they could have been reasoned with through the love of the Lord."

"I reckon there's no cure for some kinds of stupidity," Lone Wolf observed to the salesman. "Leave him lay there in the dirt, for all I care."

"You . . . you've saved our lives," Mrs. Amanda Southerby effused. She rushed to both of the men and, to Harley Goodall's utter amazement planted big, wet kisses on their cheeks.

"If you don't mind," the wounded driver called from behind them, "this is startin' to smart a bit."

Twenty minutes later, the coach started off for Memphis again. The Reverend Baker refused any treatment, glorying in his martyrdom as he whimpered in pain at each bump.

CHAPTER 12

Mrs. Amanda Southerby leaned forward in her seat and lightly tapped Harley Goodall on one knee. "If you don't mind, Mr. Goodall," she began hesitantly. "What I mean is . . . after the danger and all the excitement, that is, if it isn't too forward of me . . ."

"Yes, Mrs. Southerby?" the drummer returned mildly.

"I was wondering if I might have, you know, for medicinal purposes of course, a small bit of your elixir?"

"Why, no sooner said than done, Madam." Goodall produced a small metal cup and poured it to the rim, then handed it to the dowager. "To your very good health, Madam."

"And to yours."

They both drank deeply while the Reverend Billy Baker groaned anew and tightly shut his eyes.

"You're really quite a hero, Mr. Goodall," the buxom matron continued. "As are you, sir," to Lone Wolf, "and you, Miss Caldwell. Wherever did you learn to shoot so well?"

"In Iron . . . er, on my family's homestead in Nebraska," Rebecca replied.

"Simply marvelous. Here's to you all, then," and she hoisted her cup.

Dead highwaymen created quite a stir at the county seat at Truman. Wanted posters existed on four of the five. The money, divided between Rebecca, Lone Wolf, Goodall and the widow of the dead shotgun guard, proved substantial. With new men on the high box, the stage rattled out of the small town, southbound to Memphis.

A three day wait was in store for Rebecca when she and her companion arrived in the big Mississippi port city. They saw the sights, what there was to see, watched traffic on the river and caught up on much needed sleep. When at last the big stern wheeler hove into sight, it excited the young girl from the prairie like nothing before in her life. She had never seen such an enormous vessel, twin stacks spouting long ribbons of gray and black smoke as frothy water leaped high into the air from the big paddle bars at its stern to form miniature rainbows that hovered in arcs above the revolving boards. Small boys ran through the streets shouting and squealing with joy and Rebecca wanted to join them. A band played. Negro longshoremen gathered to move cargo. A holiday mood seized the whole town.

"Let's hurry down so we can get on board," Rebecca urged.

"You want to see the boat, that's what," Lone Wolf teased.

"What about the horses?"

"Point well taken. First on, they tell me, has first chance for a real stall."

Fifteen minutes later they met with the purser in the steam boat company's ticket office. "Two horses. Easy to accommodate," the round faced young man assured them. "Load them now if you want. Your tickets are in order?"

"Yes. We bought them two days ago," Lone Wolf told him. Rebecca's glance had wandered out to scan the busy main deck of the stern wheeler.

An hour and a half later, to still more fanfare, the *River Queen* steamed away from the docks in Memphis.

Rebecca had never been aboard any sort of boat before and the excitement she evinced ashore increased as the huge, churning paddle drove the vessel along verdant shores, lined by columns of mangrove and cypress, thickly draped with Spanish moss. The sun had nearly set on the first day of the voyage before she gave off watching the passing scene to study any of the passengers. Most seemed prosperous natives of the area, traveling on business or for a family holiday. Others, steerage passengers on the broad lower foredeck, appeared a motley lot, hardbitten farmers or laborers. Not a few Negroes appeared among the milling collection. At Lone Wolf's suggestion, she broke away from this study to check on their horses in pens on the after deck and then dress for dinner. The latter, she had discovered, was a requirement of passengers on the upper two cabin decks.

On her way down the after companionway, a young man with head bowed, intent on a message of some sort in one hand, rammed into her. The collision nearly knocked Rebecca off her feet.

"*Pardonez moi, Ma'mselle,*" the expensively dressed stranger exclaimed, extending a hand to steady her. "I am so sorry," he went on in English.

My word! She had thought Doug Fairchild quite handsome and stimulating, Rebecca considered in a flash. Yet here, this slender, smiling young man of medium stature, with wavy brown hair, glowing gray eyes and pencil-line mustache dimmed even her most ardent, intimate impressions of the young stage coach clerk. She caught her breath and she swore her heart had paused in its normal rhythm. Daintily she extended a hand to be assisted upright.

"It's all right. I'm not harmed. Thank you, sir."

"Permit me. I am Philipe DuBois of New Orleans. At your service, *Ma'mselle.*"

"I am Rebecca Caldwell, from Nebraska. This is an unusual manner of meeting, but I am . . . charmed."

"And I, too," Philipe murmured as he bent low to kiss Rebecca's hand.

A tingle of excitement ran the length of Rebecca's arm and arrowed to her palpitating breast. A matching, more earthy tremble of expectation emanated from her loins. With a start, she realized that Philipe had continued to speak.

". . . so, if *M'lle*. Rebecca is at liberty for dinner, permit me to escort you, *n'est-ce pas?*"

"Why . . ." Rebecca blurted, aflutter. "Why, I . . . ah, have no plans. None at all. I would be pleased to dine with you."

Philipe clasped his hands together and assumed a raptured expression. "You have made my day one of golden happiness, *M'lle*. Rebecca. I shall call at your stateroom at half past eight. Until then, *au revoir*."

"I . . . I'm in Seven-B," Rebecca hurried to inform him before he departed.

A wickedly engaging smile flickered on Philipe's thin lips. "That, I already know, *mon cher*."

Dinner proved to be an exciting and romantic experience. Philipe had arranged for a small table in an alcove of the main salon, snowy with crisp napery and adorned with silver appointments and candlesticks. Although bound to a vow of celibacy by his quest for spiritual power, Lone Wolf sat at a tiny, bare rectangle of hardwood bolted to the bulkhead a short distance away and glowered at Rebecca throughout. Funny, she reflected, she'd never known him to be jealous of her other, many romantic interludes. What made this different?

After a sumptuous meal, the attractive young couple took a stroll around the deck. Off across the wide expanse of the river, on both banks, small, lonesome lights marked the location of struggling tenant farmers and prosperous plantations. The first, thumbnail sliver of a new moon shone overhead and a plethora of stars frosted the high dome of night. They paused at the side rail amidship and Rebecca arranged a shawl. Deftly, Philipe slid an arm around her shoulders.

"You have taken a chill?" he inquired solicitously.

"It's the dampness off the water, I suppose," Rebecca replied in a vaguely distant voice.

"Yes. Isn't the river magnificent? We will reach Vicksburg soon. Then on to Natchez, Baton Rouge and, in four days, my home at New Orleans. So beautiful a city," he enthused. "Matched only by your own loveliness. Shall we continue our promenade . . . or would you like to . . . ?"

"Retire to your stateroom?" Rebecca completed in an eager, little girl voice. From the moment Philipe had placed his arm around her, her desire had flared into demanding need. He was deceptively strong for his size and held her with no effort against the occasional lurch and sway of the mighty vessel. "Oh, Philipe, we've hardly met . . . but . . . yes. I would very much like to go to your stateroom."

No sooner had Philipe unlocked the latch than he took her in his arms and kissed her soundly. She responded with hot abandon, their tongues flirting and exploring, probing. They entered the cabin and he secured the door. Once more they kissed, enflamed with desire.

When the embrace ended, they fumbled with burning urgency at buttons until both stood nude in the soft glow of a lowered lamp. Rebecca noticed several small, triangular scars on Philipe's lean, hard body. His engorged manhood, thick and of a pleasing length, thrust boldly out toward her, up-curved slightly, throbbing with the tidal flow of his passion. She stepped close so that it pressed against her firm abdomen, raised on tiptoes and kissed him again.

"I knew, the moment I saw you . . ." Philipe murmured when their lips parted.

"As did I." Her hand sought the rigid shaft that snuggled against her belly and encircled it with anxious fingers. She found she could not encompass it, so large was its circumference. Anticipating the effect it would have on her sensitive inner parts, she uttered a low moan of delight.

"You are pleased?" Philipe asked her as she began to lightly stroke him.

"It's so fat. I can't wait to savor its mastery of me."

"But, yes, you must."

Philipe led Rebecca to his bed and seated her upon it. Then he knelt and buried his tawny brown locks between her outstretched thighs. A tingle of incredible excitement sped through her body at the caress of his warm breath on the delicate folds of her outer portals. Then his tongue probed outward and parted the petals of her cleft. With elaborate slowness, his talented lingual muscle slathered upward until it encountered the distended pearl of her center of joy.

Nothing, no nothing, had ever been quite like this, she exulted. Wave after wave of exquisite sensations set her body to trembling as Philipe continued to circle, lave and manipulate her turgid little button with lips, tongue and teeth. She crammed a tiny fist into her mouth to stifle the shrieks of delight that rose endlessly from her core and she could see the wild palpitations of her heart against the skin of her chest. With confident ease, he withdrew, tracing his path downward until he could thrust deeply into the freely flowing passage that led to her ultimate being.

"Oh, oh, yes. There. Deeper, Philipe," she cried out. "Deeper. Fill me!"

Philipe's tongue complied, questing to extend far inside her pulsating furnace. The fingers of one hand found her breasts and began to knead them with strength and knowledge, while the others went ardently to the top of her wildly buzzing mound, to take over where his mouth had so recently given great pleasure. Rebecca wanted to leap into the air, to shout and sing and dance. Never had she felt so good.

When at last his consummate skill brought her to a crescendo, great sobbing moans tore from her inner self and trembled on her lips. Three, four, five times she shuddered mightily and convulsed in mind-blanking completion.

She lay back on the large bed and Philipe joined her, end for end. His iron-hard penis lay against her cheek and she had only to turn her head a little. Her tongue found the broad, dark red tip and began to describe spirals around it, working downward until her lips closed over the fiery shaft and she began to strenuously suck on that tree-girth of maleness.

Her passionate tremors had not even subsided before Philipe again closed his mouth over her tingling mound and cleaved her juicy slit with his avid tongue. Not even a celestial reminder of their own fleeting mortality would have dampened the avaricious pursuit of pleasure in which they engaged for more than an hour. Teasing, drawing each other up to the very crest, they quickly withdrew and let maddening sensation subside, only to coax it upward again, time after delirious time.

At last they could endure no more and they burst upon one another with fountains of primal sap.

"I have never known a man quite like you, Philipe," Rebecca panted in her post-orgasmic exhaustion.

"Nor have I encountered a woman quite like you. You have a sweetness about you, a rich, heady aroma and the taste of wild things."

"I am part Oglala Sioux."

"Aha! An entirely new experience for me. I am delighted."

"So am I. You're . . . refreshing. Exciting. Indian men know little about satisfying a woman. Their first concern is for themselves."

"Most of our race is the same, I'm sure you will find out."

"What makes you different, then?"

"I am French. The literature of my ancestors' country, its customs and teachings are all geared to provide mutual pleasure. The art of *Soixante-neuf* is carefully cultivated among the French."

"*Siox . . . ant . . .*" Rebecca's tongue twisted over the unfamiliar word.

"What we just accomplished so magnificently, my love."

Insatiable, Rebecca sought out Philipe's flaccid organ once more. She squeezed and stroked it and thrilled to its rapid response. Playfully she bent it first one way, then the next, wound it in a circle like a puppy's tail and encouraged it to full size. Then she managed to take it in both hands and begin a steady rhythm that sent shudders through his slender frame.

With a giggle of delight, she lay on her back and spread her legs.

When Philipe came to her she thought her mind would explode from the overwhelming barrage of sensations that assaulted it from the powerful presence of his enormous phallus.

It spread her.

It created new sensations in places that had never before been stimulated.

It plowed a furrow both wide and deep that sundered her inner being.

Most of all, it transported her beyond all previous realms and left her weak and trembling, while surging upward to even newer peaks.

All too soon, to Rebecca's disappointment, it had to end.

"There'll be more, my pet," Philipe promised in tender tones.

"Yes. Much more," Rebecca begged.

"There is tomorrow and tomorrow night, and two days beyond that."

"And there is tonight, beloved Philipe. Always . . . tonight."

CHAPTER 13

Two glistening bodies, leaden with satiation and damp with midafternoon passionate endeavor, separated languidly. Slowly they rose, kissed tenderly, if briefly, then began to dress.

"Tonight in the casino?" Philipe DuBois inquired.

"Yes, of course, darling," Rebecca Caldwell replied, still breathless from their last ecstatic combat.

Demure in hoop skirt and crinoline petticoats, she slipped out of Philipe's stateroom and headed for the shaded shelter of the after promenade deck. There she ordered a lemonade and sipped while the deep green river banks slid past. She longed for a bath, a luxury unavailable on the crowded paddle wheeler. She would, she decided, sponge off most thoroughly after the refreshment had cooled her. Fondly she let her thoughts drift back over her relationship with Philipe.

Through the previous two nights, and in morning and afternoon, they made love. Long, tender, fulfilling love. Inventive herself, Rebecca marveled at the vast variety of positions and devices for wilder stimulation that Philipe had in his repertoire. One, which she liked the most, was a ring of gum rubber, fitted with finger-like tendrils, which he stretched over his fat organ. It expanded even further the exploratory and stretching delights that his inexhaustible engine of love provided to her. His energy and sexual power brought her near to exhaustion. Yet, always, she quickly recharged to merge in the next clash.

What would happen to their relationship once the *River Queen* reached New Orleans? Rebecca didn't even know if Philipe was married. More to the point, she had no idea how he would react if her real mission were made known. There came moments, when she lay in his arms, that she wondered if her obsession with tracking down Jake Tulley and Roger Styles any longer had an advantage for her. She had killed several of the men involved and certainly made financial ruin of the evil pair's schemes. Unquestionably those who knew the reason for her determined pursuit had experienced terror and had their dreams haunted by her thirst for vengeance. If Philipe were to ask her to remain with him, to marry and raise a family, should she deny him? *Could* she? Then she thought of her surviving uncle.

Ezekial Caldwell. Blood kin who heartlessly turned his sister and niece over to the Oglala for their pleasure. Could she call herself whole, or clean, again until he had been made to pay for his unspeakable crime? What lawman would seek him, what court listen to the story? After all, outside Tulley and his men, *she* was the only witness. Her word against his. Swift and rude as justice had been in Tribune, Kansas, there she might look for a satisfactory verdict. But, given the sophistication of 'civilized' courts, the smoothly lying mouths of suave, clever, professional lawyers, she saw only too clearly how easily Ezekial would escape her.

He could not escape her forty-fours.

Regretfully, Rebecca formulated a new light in which to view her idyllic relationship with Philipe DuBois.

"Cards, gentlemen?" Philipe DuBois inquired of the five other players. Each of his opponents had three cards, two down, one up. They engaged in a game of *Vingt et un*, at which Philipe was an acknowledged master. *Black Jack* they called it on the frontier, Rebecca recalled. She stood behind the dashing New Orleaner with other spectators.

"One," the first man requested. He inspected the face of the five of clubs and scratched the green baise table with it to indicate a second.

The queen of diamonds. "Broke," the portly gentleman declared in a tone of disgust. He turned over all his cards, face down.

"Stand," the man on his left announced. The sandy-haired, narrow-faced man with a tiny mole at one corner of his mouth had a nine of spades showing.

"Good here," a broad, Georgia accent declared at the next spot.

"Un petite ducket, s'il vous plait," came the next request.

He received his card, though not the little one he had called for. The king of hearts. *"Cassé,"* he exclaimed, followed by a muttered curse. He folded his cards.

"I'll play these," a long legged, lean faced man drawled. His eyes had that cold, distant quality of a shootist and even his passing gaze made Rebecca uncomfortable.

Philipe set the deck aside and glanced carelessly down at the ten of clubs that showed. Then he exposed his down card, the jack of hearts. "Twenty, pay twenty-one," he announced, then repeated in French. *Vingt, j'payer vingt et un."*

"Twenty-one," the second player declared, exposing his cards. He had a toothy grin, composed of large, yellowed tombstones. His clothing, though in style, had a shabbiness about coat and trousers, a sheen where none should appear. One ear appeared to have been mangled in some terrible accident.

"Same here," the fifth man told Philipe.

Only a minutely cocked eyebrow betrayed Philipe's surprise as he set out matching sums to cover the bets.

After three more hands, the deal passed to the second man, who had been dealt a queen and ace for a natural twenty-one. "No limit stakes, boys. That's the way we like to play it," he proclaimed. His voice lacked any hint of cordiality.

"M'sieu Cortney, that is a formidable game you are proposing," the small Frenchman two players to his left remarked.

"I concur," Philipe added. "Although the cards have been running exceptionally well for you tonight. Let me order refreshments while you shuffle the cards. Gentlemen, your pleasure? *M'sieu* Dobbs, Cortney, Ralston, Jeaneau, Culhane?"

"Gineva for me," Dobbs replied.

"Bourbon," from Courtney.

"The same," Ralston contributed.

"Cognac," the fellow resident of New Orleans requested.

"Rye," Culhane declared.

"Good then," Philipe remarked as he signaled for a waiter. When the drinks arrived, the first hand had been dealt.

For over an hour, Philipe's stake continued to steadily dwindle. The fortunes of Cortney and Culhane rose with equal consistency. The fifth hand of a new shuffle went around and Philipe, as was his custom, watched each card with meticulous concentration. When Culhane declared a winner with a natural twenty-one, Philipe's hand lashed out across the table and he caught the man's wrist before he could turn the cards.

"A moment, please. I seem to recall that we had seen the ace of diamonds before in this shuffle. Odd that you should have it a second time."

"You callin' me a cheat?" Culhane growled, half rising.

Philipe's face remained a picture of genteel conviviality. "Yes, *M'sieu* Culhane, that is precisely what I am calling you. And you, too, *M'sieu* Cortney."

Well familiar with the sleight-of-hand games played by Oglala women and children, Rebecca had watched the covert manipulation of the cards, following every move. Unfamiliar with the rules of the game, she nevertheless found this suspect, particularly when it resulted in repeated wins by the two men Philipe had just accused of cheating. She had also observed an interested spectator, a small, fidgety man with thick spectacles and a walrus mustache, who peered closely at Philipe's cards over his out-sloping front and made small furtive gestures. He had repeated this on several occasions behind other players, all of whom seemed cursed with Philipe's bad luck.

She saw him tense now as the participants in the game froze around the green table.

A knife suddenly appeared in Culhane's hand. He thrust forward, with lightning speed, toward Philipe's exposed abdomen.

With equal suddenness, a Nepperhan five shot .31 caliber pocket pistol filled Philipe's fist. The hammer fell on a percussion cap and the small lead ball sped true to Culhane's right shoulder.

He dropped the knife and uttered a small groan, while blood began to well and drop tiny splatters on the green cloth table covering. Philipe recocked the diminutive pistol while he swung the barrel to cover Cortney, who had started to draw a concealed derringer. Instantly, the confidence man dropped his weapon.

Behind Philipe another weapon detonated and he swiftly glanced over his shoulder to see a short man with glasses, a big belly and walrus mustache slap his right side as though to kill a mosquito. Smoke curled from the bottom of Rebecca's silver-beaded evening purse where the blasted-open cloth revealed the muzzle of her Baby Russian. The third member of the card-sharping ring released his Remington Elliot .32 rim fire and it fell from numb fingers. His mouth sagged and a stream of blood appeared on his lips, from his punctured lungs, that ran like a cascade down his outward sloping chest.

"He tried to shoot you in the back," Rebecca calmly told Philipe.

"Mon dieu! Quoi une femme remarqueable. You have saved my life, *mon cher."* This Philipe declared as he brought his attention back to the table and the threat from Courtney.

The card cheat had disappeared. Excited voices broke out around the casino. Philipe gestured to the wounded Culhane. "You will be put in irons until we reach New Orleans, *M'sieu,* where, I warn you, a dim view is taken of card cheats. As to your accomplice behind me, I fear that the remarkable *Mademoiselle* Caldwell has rendered him *hors de combate et morte.* He is not only out of the fight," Philipe sighed and repeated in English, "but soon to be dead."

A nervous young purser approached Philipe. "Your pardon, Mister DuBois, the Captain requires some explanation of this unfortunate incident."

"Of course. At once. If you will have someone take charge of these two unfortunate villains. There is a third, calls himself Cortney, who should be easy to find."

All the questions had been answered and Rebecca lay back in the darkness of Philipe's stateroom while unending raptures sent pulses of delight along the sensitive surface of her naked skin.

Philipe's thin, bristly mustache scraped at her sparse thatch and stimulated the hyper-accented flesh of her swollen mound. His tongue, like that of a honey-dipper lapped continuously at her responsive crevice, while her legs wildly oscillated in the air in an attempt to burn off the magnificent breakers of Olympian enchantment that crashed on her nervous system.

She strained her jaw to the utmost in order to engulf his thick member, giving herself over to the delight of his manly taste. On they strived toward mutual release. Then, abruptly he left her.

Adroitly he executed a mid-bed change of direction and his vastness stretched wide her carnal passage with such force that she howled aloud in delight. The strokes began, each one stretching wider a further portion of her magical cavern. Nearly mindless with delirious joy, she strove to match him.

In the midst of their passion, the door flew open with a loud slam.

"I've got you both!" Cortney's triumphant voice bellowed. He held a large Remington .44 in one hand and a coiled bullwhip in the other.

With a wet, explosive pop, Philipe pulled free of Rebecca's fevered body and seemed to float through the air toward their would-be murderer. His left leg uppermost stuck straight out at the cardshark, the right folded back at the knee.

As the naked man hurtled down on him, Cortney blinked in amazement. Then Philipe unleashed his right leg. The arched ball of his foot struck the crooked gambler full in the chest and drove him against the door jamb. Cortney rebounded at the same moment Philipe struck the floor with both feet. Before the cowardly killer could bring up his revolver, Philipe spun to the left, a foot flying in a low arc that set off a shower of pain in Cortney's groin. He doubled over.

Philipe changed position and a solid *savate* kick with his left foot straightened up the fugitive cheat. Methodically, then, with a ferocity matched only by its eerie silence, Philipe closed in on the man who would have killed him. Cortney had dropped his Remington, though he retained his grasp on the whip. Its length suddenly snaked out behind him, then came forward with whistling speed.

The lash cut deeply into Philipe's chest. He ducked low and charged, brought a knee to Cortney's already damaged groin, then leaped back far enough for his right foot to smash into the top of the bent forward man's head.

Like a projectile from a catapult, Cortney flew across the room and smashed the mirror of an ornate dressing table. He recovered in time to lash out with the bullwhip once more.

Its lead-tipped thong ripped a ragged line two inches below Philipe's navel. He bent over, gagging and fighting to overcome the pain. Cortney heaved on the lash again, drawing blood from Philipe's back. A wild laugh broke from his lips as he sensed the kill. His big, yellow teeth glowed with cemetery phosphorescence in the light from outside.

Philipe exerted the last of his pain-numbed resources to spin and deliver a looping side-kick to the side of Cortney's head.

Staggering, the thick-shouldered confidence man reeled backward, then rolled his shoulder into another flick of the whip.

Deafening in the small cabin, Rebecca's Baby Russian blasted in the semi-darkness. Blood flew from Cortney's suddenly unhinged jaw and his assaulted ears didn't hear the second cocking of the small Smith and Wesson.

Rebecca's .38 roared again. A thin lance of flame spurted from the muzzle behind the hot, spinning bullet that punched into Robert Cortney's already deformed left ear and jellied a large portion of his brain. He reeled like a drunken man, tripped over the sill and fell dead on the outer deck, blood streaming from his mouth, nose and both ears.

"Oh, my God," Philipe gasped. "Oh, my dear God. That is twice this night you have saved my life. I owe you everything I own. All of it," he protested in empassioned Gallic effusiveness. "Never have I seen such a woman. Whatever I can do for you in New Orleans, it is yours to command. My house, my servants, my warehouses, my fortune. All is yours."

It took a great deal more explaining this time to satisfy Captain Williams.

"The Camptown darkies sing this song . . . do-dah, do-dah. The Camptown racetrack, five miles long, oh, do-dah day." To the cheerful ringing of a

banjo and the accented voices of Negro entertainers aboard the *River Queen* and on the dock, the huge stern wheeler steamed majestically toward its berth at the Esplanade Avenue wharf on the eastern end of the great horseshoe crescent of the Mississippi River that bounded the *Vieux Carre,* the French Quarter. Bright colored banners streamed in the sultry air and the shrilling of the shiny big brass whistle aboard the riverboat drowned out the cheers and music.

Amid all this jubilant chaos, enacted by the happy residents of the *Vieux Carre* since the first steamboat had plied the mighty river, Philipe stood with a possessive arm around Rebecca's shoulder and explained the sights.

"Over there, that spire. It is the bell tower of the cathedral on Jackson Square. And beside it the old Governor's Palace. There is a statue of President Andrew Jackson in the central park of the square. He saved New Orleans from the British, you know," he added. "Many fine old homes are there. Shops too. You will love my city as I love you, my dear Rebecca. There. See that carriage. That is mine. We will ride to my home and you shall stay there in state. I only wish that you had confided in me the purpose of your visit."

Rebecca hesitated. Here it was, the question she had dreaded through all the wonderful hours of their romantic tryst afloat on the Mississippi. "It . . . might hurt you, Philipe. You see, I am not all I seem."

Rebecca blushed when Philipe gave her a broad wink and fleeting smile. "Of that I am sure. But, come, it is a time to be happy. Take a deep breath, throw away your fears and tell me your secret."

Caught up in the magic of the wild moment, Rebecca did as instructed. "I came here to find two men, Jake Tulley and Roger Styles and to kill them both. My uncle Ezekial Caldwell, too, if he is with them."

Philipe gaped at this lovely young girl who had so enchantingly filled his hours of the voyage with the utmost in amorous delights. No. This he could not believe. "Surely . . . you jest?"

"No, Philipe, my dearest. I have killed four of the men who once traded me off to Indians for their own miserable hides. I don't intend to stop until each and every one of them pays."

"Then . . ." his face paled as the verity of what she said sank in. "Then, you must let me act as your champion while here. I am no mean duelist, you know. I shall encounter these villainous 'scapegraces and dispatch them to your applause."

"I . . . I'm sorry, Philipe, but I must do it myself. Don't you see?"

"No, I do not . . . Yes, I do . . . but, my dear. It simply is not done. Women do not fight duels."

"I have no intention of confronting any of them in a duel, Philipe. A shot in the back will do quite well, if necessary."

All of the color had left Philipe's face. He struck his wide, high forehead with the heel of his open palm. "*Sacre bleu!* In a trice I am fallen madly in love and then unmanned. And both by the same, most charming and lovely girl. *Alors,* I must have time to think on all of this. We will go to my city estate and rest, you, me and your friend, *M'sieu* Baylor. Then, after a fine repast this evening, we will discuss it. *Mon cher Dieu*, whatever shall be done?"

Almost aimlessly he wandered away from her to oversee the disembarkation of his many purchases upriver.

CHAPTER 14

Hotel Le Provencial fronted on Jackson Square. Its second floor rooms sported narrow, wrought-iron railed balconies that gave occupants an overview of the varied proceedings in the crowded parkland that spread out before the Cathedral and Governor's Palace. Once the *Place des Armes,* under succeeding Spanish and French colonial rule, the enlarged greensward had been planted with trees and shrubs, a fountain added, along with the statue of Andrew Jackson, erected by a grateful populace for his spirited repulse of the British in 1814.

Seated on one of these small verandahs the morning after the *River Queen* arrived were Roger Styles and Jake Tulley. They reclined backward in high-backed rattan chairs and sipped strong coffee, nibbled croissant rolls and cheese. Tulley, uncomfortable in such lavish surroundings, chafed to get back to his more familiar haunts. From what he had seen of this town, he much preferred the low dives, frequented by the town's Negro population, along Congo Square. He frowned in frustration when his big, thick fingers fumbled the small, delicate china demitasse cup.

"The good Captain should be here any time, now," Roger informed him in a languid drawl.

"He'd better be. He's suppose to have half of our money in advance on those twenty-three girls."

A knock sounded at the suite's door. "Ah, that must be him now," Roger enthused, rising to pour a fresh cup of the thick, chicory coffee.

In a moment, Luke Wellington appeared in the French doors to the balcony. "There's a man here, says he has information you ought to hear." Tall, lean and loose-limbed, the rattlesnake fast gunhawk seemed to slouch even when tautly erect.

"Who is it?"

"Didn't give a name. Said he got out of jail only an hour ago. He's got a message from an old acquaintance of yours, Mr. Styles."

"Did he say who that might be?"

"Yeah. Some feller named Liam Culhane."

"Culhane! By damn, I haven't seen, nor thought of him in three years. Send the man in, Luke."

"Yes, Mr. Styles."

Roger beamed with expectation. "You should see Culhane, Jake. He's one of the smoothest manipulators with cards you could ever encounter. An expert. Never been caught at it by anyone."

"Then why's he in jail?" Jake retorted, entirely unimpressed.

"Certainly nothing to do with his livelihood," Roger countered. "But we'll know soon enough. Come in, sir. Take a chair. Coffee?"

A gaunt-faced, tousle-haired man in his mid-thirties stood in the open doorway, hat in hand. His fingernails formed black-rimmed half moons and the clothing he wore spoke of better times. "Thank you all the same, sir. I could use a drink, though. Rum . . . or boubon? M'name's Lou Grant, I've a message for you. From a friend."

"Luke, fetch Mr. Grant a drink. Now, tell me, what of Liam Culhane?"

"He's in jail. We shared a cell over night. Said I should look you up an' tell you he's in need of one of those favors you gentlemen had stored."

Roger's eyes, despite his earlier pleasure at hearing of an old friend, narrowed in suspicion. "How did Liam know I was in New Orleans?"

"Word gets around, Squire Styles. At least amongst us that is on the dodge. Anybody's got an opportunity maybe for us sort to make a dollar, we hears soon enough. Anyway, this Liam Culhane was brought in by riverboat bulls. Seems he got caught cheatin' at cards on the *River Queen*."

"What?"

"True enough. When he heard you was about, he near went wild to get a message out of the Parish Prison back o' Congo Square. He said to tell you he'd been hearin' things of late about you and a gentleman named Tulley." Shrewd eyes twinkled with calculation when Grant saw a quick glance pass between the two men. "He said you'd pay him well for the information an' . . ." Grant hesitated a fraction of a second. "An' me, too, for bringing you word."

"What is this valuable information?"

Grant accepted a half tumbler of bourbon, gulped deeply and wiped a grimy hand over his mouth to collect dribbles. "It has to do with a girl named Rebecca Caldwell. He didn't say any more." Avarice glowed in his weak, watery blue eyes.

Styles and Tulley blanched a moment, then the outlaw boss flushed a beet hue and half-rose from his chair. "That bitch!" he growled.

Lou Grant knew he had scored a few cartwheels. He licked his chapped lips and drank again from the whiskey. "That's all he tol' me. Said I was to let you know where he was and that he knew something about this Rebecca Caldwell. Uh . . . I, ah, ain't got anything else to relate. So, I'll, ah, take my leave." He slugged down the last of the bourbon while hesitantly extending his other hand, empty palm up.

To Lou Grant's utter surprise, Roger Styles dropped three ten dollar coins into his hand. The gold had a soft, seductive glow. Quickly the derelict made them disappear into a pocket of his baggy trousers. "Thank you, Squire Styles. Any time I can render you a service."

"Of course. Now leave us."

After Grant had been ushered out by Luke Wellington, Styles turned to Tulley. "First thing, we arrange with a judge I have in my pocket to get bail for Culhane. Then we find out what it is he knows. Let's head for the Parish Prison."

Liam Culhane winced at the pain in his shoulder. The police doctor had redressed the wound, though conditions in the dank stone cells of the fortress-like prison had started it to festering. He greeted Roger

Styles with a wry smile.

"I thought you would never get caught," Roger joked.

"Don't remind me. I wouldn't have if it hadn't been for a New Orleans dandy named Philipe DuBois and . . . a girl named Rebecca Caldwell."

"You saw her? Where?"

"On the *River Queen.*"

Styles seemed incredulous. "She's here? In New Orleans?"

"Yes, damned luck for me. There'll be a trial. One of my partners tried to even things up. The Caldwell woman blew his brains out."

"Don't worry about a trial," Roger assured him. "From now on you are working for me. Now I have to figure out how to take care of that pesty Rebecca."

It took only a few questions for Roger to find directions to the person he wanted to consult. He went to a small shop on Orleans Street, where a sign declared that the proprietoress sold *herbals* and other salutary plants. He stepped through the glass-paned door and a dangling collection of short, bleached bones above it rattled an announcement of his presence.

Malvina Latour, a *cafe au lait* mulatto, was a composed person, with exceedingly handsome features and a fine, fully developed figure. She wore her favorite costume, a dress of blue calico with white dots and, on her head, a brilliant orange-colored Madras handkerchief. Her long, black hair had been done in a radical upsweep and entirely contained inside the *tignon*. Born a free woman of color, as were most who pursued her line, her brother had become a member of the "black-and-tan" Legislature installed in the newly purchased Saint Louis Hotel by the Reconstruction Government, which had converted the old hostelry into the new state capitol. She greeted her white visitor with cool self-possession.

"You come for a *gris-gris?* Or an ox-heart charm, sah?"

"For neither," Roger Styles told her. "I need to consult the Voodoo Queen."

"I am she. What is your problem?"

"I expected you to know that, if your reputation does not exceed the reality."

"It concerns a woman. A young woman, no?"

Roger smiled. "It does indeed." Quickly he explained what he wanted.

"This I can not do for you. I do not like sending a person in need to one who is barely more than a jungle witch doctor, but I must in this case. You should seek an audience with Doctor James Alexander. That is a *Voodoo Magnian* title. He's not a real doctor. He is located at a fine house on Monroe Street, near Royal. It is better that you visit him there instead of his office here on Orleans. He is a Voodoo Doctor, sells charms by mail. He also engages in the dark rites you desire."

"Thank you, your Majesty."

"My title is *Mamma Loa,* Mr. Styles."

"T-thank you, *Mamma Loa,*" Roger intoned in feigned reverence. Only a slight stammer betrayed his shock at her use of his name, though he had not introduced himself.

They had come to an agreements of sorts. Rebecca

remained implacable in her determination to hunt down Jake Tulley and Roger Styles. Philipe insisted she put it aside for a while and consider marriage and a home with him. She stayed the night at his townhouse, then moved into the Hotel Maison DuPrix on Toulouse Street. Philipe had insisted she stay away from the more fashionable hotels near Jackson Square due to the recent agitations by the White League, a group dedicated to breaking the oppressive yoke of Reconstruction government-by-fiat. Lone Wolf resided there, too. He settled in his room and then went out around the town to seek some lead to the men they pursued. Rebecca's great worry was that they would be gone. Time wasted, that could never be recovered. All the same, while she, too, made quiet inquiries, she arranged to meet Philipe for lunch.

They dined on crayfish, prawns and a variety of creole dishes, including red beans and rice. Philipe pursued his urgent suit and won an agreement from her to have dinner and go dancing with him. They parted company and Rebecca strolled into Jackson Square.

Cart vendors seemed to be everywhere, selling nearly anything a person could want, from religious medallions and votive candles to live ducks, dried fish and coffee beans. She paused in front of the Cathedral and studied the ornate Spanish Colonial architecture. Smeared on the walls were some crudely printed posters signed by the White League Philipe had mentioned. They called for "freedom" from the corruption and degredation of the "black-and-tan" rump Legislature.

"There she is. Damnit, I don't believe it, but there, see her over by the church," Jake Tulley whispered excitedly to Luke Wellington.

The rangy blond gunhawk peered down from the balcony of the Hotel Le Provencial at the throng and recognized the trim form of Rebecca Caldwell, despite the stylish clothing she wore. "You're right, boss."

"Take three of the boys and go get her. We haven't time to wait around for Roger's fancy ideas to work out."

"Right away."

Even in a crowd, the lessons she had learned living with the Oglala set a warning going in Rebecca's mind. Faces that didn't belong. That impression registered first. Two men, headed in her direction, worked their way through the clots of people with determination. Their fixed expressions further alarmed her. She turned away from them and started to ease a path through the chattering women and bartering vendors. A quick glance showed that the men altered direction to match hers. She started walking faster, her right hand tightly gripped the butt of the Baby Russian in her purse. A darkly shaded alleyway on the east side of the square caught her attention.

A plan formed as she headed toward the narrow opening.

Once inside the alley, she broke into a shuffling trot that quickly carried her two thirds of the way through to the next street. She ducked into a recessed doorway and cast a brief glance back the way she had come. The brightness of the square blotted out as two figures entered the passage and started her way.

"She musta run through to the other street," one panting hardcase remarked.

"That's all right. Luke an' Curley are over there."

They drew closer and Rebecca took out her small revolver. When they trotted past, without even a look, she stepped out into the alley behind them. "Hello, boys," she said in a small, demure voice.

They wheeled about in awkward surprise.

"Did Jake send you after me?"

In the dimness they did not see her .38 Smith and Wesson. Instantly they leaped toward her, arms out to make the capture.

Rebecca rammed the muzzle of the Baby Russian in the nearer one's belly and squeezed the trigger.

His soft beer gut muffled the sound of the shot. Hot gasses from the burnt powder rushed through the ragged entry wound and expanded disastrously among his intestines. Ripped apart, they spilled their putrid contents into his abdominal cavity. His eyes bulged and Rebecca stepped back from the falling corpse. A hand caught at her left wrist.

Rebecca swung her right arm over and shoved the muzzle of the revolver under her attacker's chin. He had only enough time to register that fact before a hot .38 slug ripped up through his tongue and entered the lower portion of his brain with a spray of bone chips, blood and searing vapors. Black powder smoke wisped from his ruptured ears and streamed from his nose.

Damn, Rebecca thought as she hurried back to the populated square. Now she was no better off than before. She still had no idea where Jake and Roger could be hiding.

Doctor Alexander, a tall, slim mulatto from Mississippi, looked over long, steepled fingers at the white man on the other side of his small desk. Beside him sat his associate, Doctor Sol, otherwise known as Solomon Hastings, and to one side, Annie Gould, his constant companion and, though a freed slave a competent secretary. Around the room the grisly tools of his trade served to make Roger Styles decidedly uncomfortable.

A score of human and dog skulls rested on knick-knack shelves, or adorned table tops and bookshelves. Hundreds of dusty jars contained dried snakes, lizards, frogs and horned toads. A huge, fat, living snake, of a breed unfamiliar to Roger, lay torpid in a window seat, its middle distended by its recent feast of a pudgy puppy. The tip of the unfortunate meal's tail still protruded from the serpent's lipless mouth.

"I's understand dis cor-rect, yous wants dis white gal to be cotched up offen de streets an' done in by some means dat can't never be traced to yo'-all. Dat de right ob it?"

"Precisely correct, Doctor Alexander. I was given to, ah, understand that you had a particular use for such, ah, persons. Something to do with your worship of Dumbala?"

"We's don' go inta details about such goin's on. Exspecial wif offays lak yo'sel'. Yo' pay de fee fo' a service an' we does as we lak wit de lef'ovahs."

Roger suppressed a shudder that ran on frozen cat

feet up his spine. "And what would that, ah, fee amount to?"

"Would fitty dollah be 'bout right?"

A sigh of relief hissed through Roger's nostrils. He'd expected a great deal more. "That would be fine. With a bonus of another, ah, fifty if the body is never found."

"Done. Pleasure doin' business wif yo'all. Jis gib de money to Miz Gould heah."

Champagne made her giggle. Rebecca learned this at their first stop that evening. A table of ornate hors d'oeuvres graced one side of the enclosed patio at the exclusive restaurant where Philipe escorted her. They munched on various viands and sipped from never empty glasses of sparkling wine amid the soft, cultured conversation of their fellow diners.

"You seem to do rather well, regardless of the Reconstruction," Rebecca remarked, glancing around at the expensively dressed patrons of the establishment.

"Fortunately, New Orleans did not suffer the same fate as so many Southern cities. The North's General Hooker found the *Vieux Carre* to be enchanting. Particularly the ladies of loose virtue. Instead of razing the town, he ordered it guarded."

"And so life goes on."

"Is anything the matter, Rebecca?" Philipe asked with genuine concern. "When I called for you at the DuPrix, you appeared a bit pale and upset."

"It's nothing. No, that's not true, Philipe. Perhaps

". . . if I tell you, then you will understand why I can and will do this thing myself."

"Tell me what, for heaven's sake?"

"Two of Tulley's gunmen spotted me this afternoon. They followed me into that small alley off the east side of Jackson Square."

Shock and confusion registered on Philipe's face. "But why would you go in there?"

"To catch them and find out where Tulley and Styles are holding up. Anyway, they tried to grab me so . . . I killed them."

Philipe blanched. "Two, ah, I gather, armed men? You killed them both?"

"Yes. Now do you see that I am capable of caring for myself. Others have tried to help in the past, dear Philipe. Far too many times it resulted in their deaths at the hands of Tulley's gunslingers, or in horrible wounds. I spent five years among some of the cruelest people in the world. The Oglala know of no other life than survival. You learn to fight for what's yours or you don't live long. I'm suited to go after animals like Tulley because what he did to me made me into a sort of animal, too."

Philipe placed a hand lovingly over both of hers, imprisoning them and stilling her protestations. "Let's not talk of such dark things tonight, *non?* We will be carefree and gay and let the world go on without us."

They had eaten, gone on to a small private cotillion and returned to Rebecca's hotel room at one in the morning. It took little time for them to remove their stiff, formal clothing.

Rebecca ran her hands over the silken sheen of

Philipe's lean, hard body. She bent to kiss every small, puckered scar, emblems of his career as a duelist. His breath grew rough and his thick penis stood valiantly out from his body, rigid with desire and dew-tipped with readiness. Lastly, Rebecca knelt and kissed away the clear jewel that hovered on the dark red tip. Philipe produced her favorite, the many-fingered rubber device, and she slipped it over his vastness.

Philipe lifted her and carried her to the bed. He lowered the lamps and joined her. His skillful fingers manipulated her nether parts until they vibrated with slippery invitation. With a smooth motion he situated himself between her wide-spread legs and lowered his pulsating member to the gates to paradise.

"Oh, God, Philipe!" Rebecca cried out as the hard, fat tree trunk entered her. "Oh-oh-oh . . . YES!"

In the deeply slumbering hour before dawn, four figures, blacker than the shadows through which they flitted, approached the rear entrance to the Maison DuPrix hotel on Toulouse Street. Another silent figure, a negress maid named Lila, let them in.

Stealthily they climbed to the second floor. There they paused before going up a narrow, spiral staircase to the garret rooms above. One produced a key and opened the third door in the short hallway.

On the bed inside, utterly drained and sated from three hours of exotic loving, Rebecca Caldwell lay sprawled in her golden-glowing nakedness. White teeth flashed in black faces as the intruders exchanged lusty smiles. One of them produced a small bottle and a wad of cotton, doused the batting and the odor of chloroform filled the room.

" 'Member," the leader cautioned. "No body gwine fuck her. We's jist gonna steal her."

CHAPTER 15

"She's gone," Lone Wolf growled like a Rocky Mountain grizzly. "This is the way I found the room this morning," he went on to Philipe DuBois.

"We will have to notify the police."

"If it will do any good. There were men here. Three, maybe four. Buffalo Heads," he added, using the Crow name for Negroes.

"Then I know where we can start looking," Philipe declared after the name had been explained. "We'll go to Mammy Sue Picard."

"Do you have a gun?"

Philipe patted his coat. "Right here."

"I mean something that will stop a man with one shot?"

"Not with me."

"Take one of Rebecca's Smith Americans, then. And a pocket full of ammunition."

Twenty minutes later Lone Wolf and Philipe entered a small, three-room clapboard house on Roman Street. A grossly fat old woman sat on a sagging leather chair. Her gray hair had been neatly tucked into a white *tignon* and she had cut away the sides of a pair of shoes to hold her large feet. The dress she wore was clean, but faded, a once-blue frock of considerable quality. Philipe made the introductions.

"Mammy Sue, we've come on an important matter. A young woman I care a great deal about has been taken away by some local nigras. We need someone who can look into it without creating a problem."

"So youse come to me. When an' from where was she taken?"

"Early this morning," Lone Wolf provided. "From the Hotel Maison DuPrix."

"We believe that some white men may have been involved. Paid the boys for taking her."

"In dat case, youse needs to see the *Momma Loa.*"

"Who is that?" Lone Wolf inquired.

"The Voodoo Queen," Philipe explained. "Do you think this has anything to do with Voodoo rituals?"

"Might. Then again it might not." Mammy Sue raised one chubby hand and mopped at the perspiration on her brow. "Thing like this . . . you never know. Go see Malvina."

Outside on the street, Philipe filled Lone Wolf in on the old lady they had visited. "Mammy Sue used to be a slave on my family's place. She was freed long before the War and has lived here since. We look in on her from time to time, see she has what is needed. She's very loyal and if she says that Voodoo is involved, you can bet it is true."

"But this . . . Voodoo. What is it?"

"A form of African religion that came here through slaves from Martinique, Guadeloupe and Santo Domingo. They had originated on the Guinea Coast.

The real power in Voodoo is the Queen. Malvina Latour is the present one." His voice turned sour. "Her brother is a 'black-and-tan'. He's been helping make a muddle out of state government since the Reconstruction Yankees stuffed him and his like in the Legislature and cast out all of the whites. But that's another story. Malvina has a shop on Orleans. We'll go there."

"Ah! Mis-tah DuBois," Malvina Latour greeted when he and Lone Wolf entered the shop. "What brings you to my humble little store?"

"I need to know something. Are your people planning any rituals right now?"

"N-no. Not those who consult with this person at any rate."

"Please, this is important. Don't be evasive," Philipe appealed, one hand nervously ruffling his wavy brown hair.

"You might shuffle down the street to Doctor Alexander's shop. Those fools who listen to him say there's big doin's in the works."

"Thank you, *Momma Loa,*" Philipe said breathlessly. He dropped some gold coins in the small brass bowl on a side counter.

Doctor Alexander's *Herbal Medicine* shop was empty. The locks had been set and blinds half-drawn. In frustration, Philipe shook the doorknob.

"Let me," Lone Wolf offered. He located some burlap bags in a refuse barrel beside the neighboring green grocer. These he wrapped around his Remington to muffle the noise and pressed the muzzle to one lock.

A flat report sounded and a screen of powder smoke spread from the sacks. Lone Wolf repeated the process on the second lock. With a loud, metallic grinding, the door opened. Lone Wolf put the smoldering gunny sacks in the trash can and together, he and Philipe entered the store.

"What do we look for?" Philipe asked in his helplessness.

"Anything that might tell us something."

Bottles and jars, filled with the noxious products used in the black arts, lined shelves behind a counter. Cruets of foul-smelling oils sat near a wooden cash drawer. Dust lay heavily over most of the items. At the back door, Lone Wolf found bare footprints in the layer of tan grit. Four sets.

"The Buffalo Heads again," he pointed out to Philipe. He continued his search, making use of all the skills ten years with the Crow had taught him.

In one corner the grime had been recently disturbed by a large object that had laid on the floor. On closer examination, Lone Wolf located a thin strip of tanned, white leather.

"Doeskin fringe from Rebecca's dress," he told Philipe.

"But why would they trouble to dress her in that?"

"If Tulley and Styles are involved, it has great meaning to them. As a captive of the Sioux, Rebecca wore white-bleached doeskin dresses. She still prefers them for the comfort. If nothing else, they would want all such things to disappear with her. Supposing they intend to watch whatever Alexander has in store for her, it could have some symbolic purpose for them. At least we know that she was here. Now we must find where she was taken."

Back at Malvina Latour's shop, the Voodoo Queen studied on the matter for a few moments. "In the old days, such things were done in huts along Congo Square. Then in the old brickyard. Now, my followers meet to celebrate feasts and other rituals in a small chapel on the banks of Lake Pontchartrain. There is another place, one far removed from our chapel, where such practices are followed. It is deep into the swampy ground at the lake. Not even I know how to find it."

"We'll go back to Mammy Sue," Philipe decided.

"We're well rid of that bitch now," Jake Tulley gloated when a representative of Doctor Alexander had departed after reporting on the successful kidnapping.

"With the loss of two more men who didn't need to die," Roger snapped. "If you had left it up to me, that wouldn't have happened."

"Captain Decker," Luke Wellington announced, interrupting their heated words.

"Show him in, Luke," Roger commanded.

Captain Orsen Decker of the four thousand ton steam-sailer *Moroney* entered with a seadog's sway to his walk. His girth nearly matched his height, which was below average. He had a brutal face, scarred with an old knife-slash, pig eyes and thick, pouting lips, of an offensive livery color. A wide leather belt, studded with knives and a pair of old-fashioned boarding pistols, encompassed his huge beer belly.

"You weren't here yesterday," he accused in a rumbling bear voice.

"Business," Roger dismissed. "Drink, Captain?"

"Rum if ye've got it." He accepted the glass.

"You brought the money?" Jake Tulley asked with avarice.

"Of course, ye blinkin' idiot. Right here." He slapped his thick middle. "I'll tell ye, lads, them potentates over there have had stiff peckers since the moment I described the, ah, cargo we had for 'em. They been humpin' their donkeys and buggerin' little boys for so long they can't wait to get their hands on something fresh and new."

"So how much more did they pay?" Roger inquired, his own greed overcoming his breeding.

"I can't believe this myself, but when I described all those hairless little pussies and the tiny little tits, they upped the ante by fifty dollars each. We all gonna be rich men," the boorish captain enthused.

"Not nearly so rich as I desire to be, Captain Decker," Roger returned coolly. "This little enterprise is only a sideline for me."

"Don't overlook the considerable risk it is to me, lads. Why if the authorities caught wind of those little girls on my ship, I'd lose it and me sailin' papers and do more time in jail than there is years before the Second Coming."

"No one will ever know. And after you've conducted your business with us, I'm certain you'll find others in, ah, need of ready cash money to enliven your dirty little practice for many a long year."

Decker grumbled. "Then, there's my first mate to take care of. Mr. Godfrey purports to be a religious man and it ain't easy to bend his stubborn back when it comes to escapades like this."

"More likely you got to keep his hands off the merchandise, else it arrive in a spoiled condition, eh?" Roger chortled.

Decker winked. "That's the right of it, though I hate to admit it."

"Well, then, Captain, let's get to the distribution of the rewards," Roger urged.

The sun had slanted far over toward evening before Philipe and Lone Wolf located the old man to whom Mammy Sue had sent them. He indeed had a pirogue available and knew the circuitous route through the torturous mangrove swamp to the chapel used by Doctor Alexander for his orgiastic rites. For a fee, he would guide them. To the old Negro's suprise, Lone Wolf loaded some unusual equipment into the low sided boat.

"The bow lets us get in close and do some silent work," he told Philipe. He indicated his Crow warbow and quiver of arrows. "You have your rifle and the Parker. Also Rebecca's Smith and Wesson. We don't want to take chances, but I won't mourn if none of the Voodoo people come out of this alive. If Styles and Tulley aren't out there, we still have to track them down. Keep low and we'll figure out how to attack when we see what we're up against."

With a grunt, the old man shoved off and paddled toward the head of the small stream that originated in Lake Pontchartrain.

CHAPTER 16

For the third time that day, Rebecca awakened. She had been drugged. That much she could recall. First there had been the men who broke into her room. And a strong, sickening odor. She had tried to struggle when they put the cotton over her mouth and nose. Then blackness. She remembered a dusty floor in a small smelly shop of some sort. Once more she had been forced into unconsciousness. Now, the rhythmic patter of some sort of small drums had dragged her back to reality. Her present surroundings were far more disturbing than any before.

A cautious look around made her aware she lay on some sort of oblong table, perhaps eight foot by four in size. She raised her head and, at the far end, saw a black cat. At first she thought it alive, then realized it must be a stuffed one. By craning her neck, she saw a white cat poised over her head. At the center, near her narrow waist, she saw a cypress sapling, some four feet in height, planted in the center of a small wooden keg. Immediately behind it, against a wall of widely spaced slats, was a black doll with a dress decorated with cabalistic signs and strange emblems. A necklace of what appeared to her to be snake vertebrae hung around the doll's neck, with some sort of fang encased in silver for a pendant. *Where was she?* The question nagged her.

By straining, she could see the drummers. Two Negro women tapped on small tam-tams with heads made of vari-colored snake skin. Beside them, a tall, slim Negro man sat astride a cylindrical drum with a sheepskin head. With two sticks he pounded on it with a monotonous *ra-ta-ta, ra-ra-ta-ta*. To Rebecca, it appeared the sticks could be the thigh bones of an animal, or perhaps a small human. A short distance away, a young, light-skinned negress beat an accompaniment with a pair of leg bones. A shudder ran through her at the sound of this weird, satanic discord. Sudden the scrawny drummer leaped to his splayed bare feet and whirled out into the center of the room

"Houm! Dance Calinda! Voudou! Magnian! Aie! Aie! Dance Calinda!" He shouted the chant in some long-forgotten African tongue.

More people began to appear in her scope of vision. Mostly women, a few men intermingled into a circle of black, half-naked bodies that began to stamp and sway in time to the unearthly music and rotate counter-clockwise in front of the table where Rebecca lay. The women were all dressed in elaborate costume, some of them in bridal gowns. The men wore only thin, cotton underdrawers and Rebecca could see the bulge of their erections. Gradually the tempo of their dance increased. At the center of the ring, the rail-thin Negro was being attended by two women, who removed his baggy underdrawers and proceded to rub him all over with some pungent oil. In the flickering of twin fires, one at each open end of the two wall enclosure, he glistened like some supernatural being. He raised his hands above his head and called out in a mellifluent voice.

"A present commencez!" he began, speaking the local French patois. Then he recited a strange poem that meant nothing to Rebecca.

> *"Malle couri dan deser,*
> *Malle marche dan savane,*
> *Malle marche su piquan dore,*
> *Malle oir ca ya di moin!*
>
> *"Sange moin dan l'abitation ci la la?*
> *Mo gagnain soutchien la Louisiane,*
> *Malle oir ca ya di moin!"*

As he chanted his incarnation, he seemed to grow in height and breadth and his eyes rolled in a sort of wild frenzy. There was hate and ferocity in every word, boldness and defiance in each gesture. Rebecca had no words to name this ritual of madness, enmity and lust. The women began to tear at their clothes, rending them and hurling the bits away from the circle, until they were quite naked. Aroused to unbelievable heights of sexual ferment, the males divested themselves of their single piece of clothing.

They formed an outer ring and began to jerk and twist their bodies and strut in the opposite direction of the wildly gesticulating women, with movements that reminded Rebecca of chickens in a barnyard. At the apex of their frenetic, sensual performance, Doctor Alexander made his appearance.

He stood on the unmortared brick hearth where one fire burned, dressed in a tall beaver hat and a goatskin loincloth, so arranged that his huge, vibratingly erect penis thrust out through the animal's mouth. Women screamed and frothed at the mouth and some fell in a dead faint. In his left hand he held a gourd rattle, which he shook in time with the music. In his right he grasped a large French vegetable knife. Firelight made a blue line of its wickedly sharp edge. He advanced on the dancers and they fell back, arms waving hypnotically over their heads.

His acolytes, naked young black girls of twelve or so, ran forward with calabash cups and administered the Voodoo sacrament these contained to the reveling worshipers. What next? Rebecca wondered as she struggled at the bonds that held her firmly on the table.

"We's gettin' close," the old man whispered to Lone Wolf. "Hear de drums?"

Ten minutes later, the pirogue grounded silently on a tufted mound that rose out of the swamp. The guide tied off to a cypress knee that stood up from the water and held the craft steady while Lone Wolf and Philipe clambered out. "Dey's plenty time. De new doktah dey's makin' tonight ain't called out de *Voodoo Magnian*. You go along dat little path, find de chapel. Mebbe quarter mile."

"Good. You'll wait here for us?" Lone Wolf inquired.

"Oh, yassah. I waits like Mammy Sue tole me."

Cautiously, the two men advanced along the dimly marked trail toward the growing sound of drums. Past a stand of cypress, they made out the yellow glow of a fire. Lone Wolf crouched low and, imitating him, Philipe followed suit. They crept to within a hundred yards of the gap-sided drying shed used for Voodoo ceremonies and hunkered down to study the situation.

"We'll go in from each end," Lone Wolf planned aloud. "Shoot everything that moves, unless they're running away. But watch out for Rebecca."

"No problem on that, *mon ami.* I will be quite careful for her sake. Most of these Voodoo followers are women. I doubt that they will offer much resistance."

"Any who do, kill them," the former Crow brave answered coldly.

Doctor Alexander entered the circle and stood before the slim, light-skinned man who writhed about and babbled in some incomprehensible language. Alexander raised the gourd rattle and shook it violently. The entranced Negro fell silent.

"Anton Sade," Dr. Alexander intoned in a jumble of Orleans French and African Guinea dialect, "you are about to become *Voodoo Magnian,* a Doctor of dark secrets and mighty powers. How do you wish to be known?"

"Doctor Calinda," Anton replied. His vacant eyes became fixed on the huge knife in Doctor Alexander's hand and his senses reeled.

Born thirty-one years earlier, Anton Sade had grown up on a plantation near Baton Rouge. He had run away at the age of fourteen and lived with a young free woman of color in New Orleans for some years. She had introduced him to Voodoo and he quickly became enthralled with its orgiastic aspects. He had applied himself to the study of the verbal history of Voodoo and knew all the spells, chants and formulas for making potions. With each advance in his skill, the young mulatto's zeal grew nearer to obsession. Now he stood on the threshold of his most coveted accomplishment.

Doctor Alexander took a gourd cup from one trembling girl, who could not keep her eyes off his engorged organ thrust boldly outward. He drank from it and lifted the edge to Anton Sade's lips. When both had sipped from it, he passed it back to the child, who scurried from the circle.

"To pass over from mere man to Doctor Calinda, you must make sacrifice to *Dumbala*. A blood sacrifice, in three parts. Here is the instrument of your transformation." Doctor Alexander handed Anton the knife.

A woman darted into the circle bearing a chicken in both hands. Anton seized the bird and slashed off its head. A fountain of blood sprayed his naked flesh and the hard-packed dirt floor.

When the chicken twitched its last, two small, naked boys, one black, the other white, led forward a goat. Again the giant knife swung and the goat's head fell with a wet thud. Gore spattered over the dancers.

"And now, the final, great sacrifice," Doctor Alexander declared.

Swaying, their bare feet making slapping sounds on the ground, Doctor Alexander and Anton Sade walked toward the table where Rebecca lay. Sade licked droplets of blood from his lips and raised the blade.

Lone Wolf reached his position a moment after the dance began. He peered through the fire's glare at the bizarre interior. At first he did not locate Rebecca, then saw the table set out like some sort of primitive altar. She lay on it, bound hand and foot. When the tall black man appeared and brought the knife to another in the center of a circle of dancers, Lone Wolf nocked an arrow and waited for a clear shot.

The killing of the chicken and goat startled and puzzled him. When the two men began to walk toward the table and the recumbent form of Rebecca Caldwell, he realized only too well the purpose they had in mind. Lone Wolf drew the bowstring back to his ear and took careful aim.

The eerie whistle of the fletchings reached Doctor Alexander's ears a fraction of a second ahead of the meaty smack when the arrow's sharp point buried deeply in Anton Sade's right shoulder. A scream of sheer agony escaped the slender mulatto and he dropped to his knees. Lone Wolf launched another shaft, then a third.

Two more of the Voodoo cultists crumpled to the ground. They writhed and groaned, hands clasped to the shafts that protruded from their stomachs.

Shots blasted out of the night from the opposite end of the shed and pandemonium erupted among the worshipers. Women screamed and ran in purposeless circles. Others dived for the floor. A man clasped a hand to his forehead and uttered a thin wail before he crumpled and lay in a spreading pool of blood.

Lone Wolf opened fire with his Winchester, aiming for the men among the congregation.

First one fell, then another. Wild cries of terror filled the night.

Doctor Alexander forgot entirely about his wounded protege. He bolted from beside the table and ran for the distant opening. A bullet ticked his goatskin loincloth and he yowled in horror at the thought of losing his manhood.

"Allez! Allez!" Philipe yelled, as though commanding a band of men. He ran directly at Doctor Alexander, who batted wildly at him and fled off into the darkness. "After them, men!" the young man bellowed, enjoying his role.

"Kill them all!" Lone Wolf roared, then emitted his paralyzing Crow warcry and raced into the shed.

Rebecca felt the weight of the knife on her hand and wiggled her fingers until she maneuvered it into position. A gentle, sawing motion with her wrist and she freed that arm. Quickly she grasped the handle of the kitchen tool and cut through her other bonds. A light of cold fury glowed in her dark blue eyes. When she swung her legs over the edge of the table, Anton Sade saw that glint of rage and shrieked in falsetto terror.

With a powerful swing, Rebecca brought the knife down.

Sade dodged, though not fast enough. His left ear lay on the ground at his side. Another howl of anguish tore from his throat. Rebecca dropped lightly to the hard-packed earth and wielded the blade a second time.

A new, rosy grin spread from Anton's whole right ear to his savaged left. The lips peeled back so that a froth of bloody bubbles hissed out of his severed throat. His eyes went wide, showing mostly white, and he clutched at the fatal gash with both hands. A moment later, Philipe DuBois reached Rebecca's side.

"I'll get you out of there."

Her abduction and rough handling, the horror of the Voodoo ritual and her near brush with death had raised Rebecca's blood lust. "No. I want to kill them all."

"Hurry, there are only your friend Baylor, myself and you. If they rally and realize that, we could all be killed."

Lone Wolf pelted up. "Hurry, Rebecca, we have to get out of here."

"All . . . all right." She saw the .44 American in Philipe's belt and pulled it free. With methodical determination, she pumped two slugs into Anton Sade's corpse. Then she shot a yelling man who ran toward them with a cane knife. He was, she recalled, one of those who had taken her from the hotel.

"Now we can go," she told her rescuers.

Back out of the swamp, Rebecca again wearing her doeskin dress, the trio sat at a table in Mammy Sue's kitchen.

"They's bad folks, them Voodooers," Mammy Sue muttered as she prepared coffee.

"We still have to find Tulley and Styles," Rebecca told the others.

"How would children be taken from New Orleans to some other place?" Lone Wolf speculated out loud.

"By riverboat," Philipe suggested.

"No, that could have been arranged up-river, since they had to be brought across country in the first place," Rebecca argued. "That way there would have been no reason to come to New Orleans."

"What about by ship?" Philipe offered. "They come and go from here to all parts of the world."

"Yes. At the docks. Sooner or later, Roger Styles will have to talk to whoever he's working with. We can watch the docks."

"First, we can all use some rest," Lone Wolf suggested.

"That can come later," Rebecca told them. "When they learn that the Voodoo people didn't kill me, Tulley will send men hunting. We have to take the fight to them."

CHAPTER 17

"In another words, you make a fucking mess out of it," Roger Styles growled at an abashed Doctor Alexander. The two men, and Jake Tulley, stood in the center of the livingroom of Roger's suite at the Le Provencial.

"Dat is a mighty harsh remark, Mistah Styles."

"None the less true, however. I expect the money I paid you to be returned."

Alexander turned a muddy gray. "We's done earned dat money."

"How? By allowing Rebecca Caldwell to escape? Pay up or I'll turn Jake's boy loose on you."

"My Voodoo powers will protec' me from dem."

"They didn't do much for your boys, Anton Sade, when Lone Wolf put an arrow in him," Roger sneered.

"It were dat she-devil what done cut his throat," Alexander said defensively.

"Pay me, you nigger fraud, or you'll not walk out of here alive."

Jake Tulley loosened the Colt revolver in his holster.

Reluctantly, with a shrug of resignation, Doctor Alexander withdrew a large roll of bills from his pocket and began to count them out. Roger put a hand on his and stopped the procedure.

"In gold, same as I paid you. Those foldin' dollars aren't worth the paper they're printed on."

Alexander put away the wad of cash and took out a small leather bag. From it he counted two double-eagles and a ten dollar gold piece. "Fitty dollah. Jist lak I got it from yo'."

"Thank you, Doctor," Roger replied in a snide tone. "Always a pleasure doing business with you. Now, Luke, get his black ass out of here," he ended with a growl.

After Doctor Alexander had been ejected, Roger paced the floor a moment. He paused to peer through the louvered slats of the shutters at clots of men gathering in Jackson Square. Angry mutters rose from the street. Then he turned back to Tulley.

"If you were Rebecca Caldwell, what would you do now, Jake?"

"I'd come looking for the two of us," Jake replied ungrammatically.

"I'm afraid you are right, Jake. On both counts. I should have let your boys hunt her down. That's what we'll have to do now. Get your men out there and have them comb the streets."

"At night?"

"Hell yes, 'at night'. Do yo think she's gonna wait around until morning and politely send in her calling card?"

"All right, all right. But what about that mob gathering outside?"

"They have nothing to do with us. I heard earlier it's a protest against the rump Legislature of darkies that occupy the state capitol. Get your men moving."

"Sure, Roger. Then, what are we going to do?"

"I've taken consideration of that. With that girl and her white savage companion here, it must mean they know all about the wagon loads of girls. They may have already dealt with that, or are expecting to get us first and then free the girls when they get here. Either way, I think we should take passage with our good friend, Captain Decker. Wherever we go, at least we will be away from Rebecca Caldwell."

"What about Zeke? He's supposed to meet us here."

"Let him fend for himself. Now get moving on hunting her down."

Philipe DuBois' coach rolled along Canal Street, the clop of hoofs and grate of iron tire rims loud in the early morning hours. They would drive straight down to the public docks and start their search from there. At the sound of the approaching vehicle, two men stepped into the dark shadows under an overhanging balcony.

"Look in that carriage, Lyle. Don't that gal look like the one we's supposed to find?"

"Where?" Lyle paused, peered in the direction pointed out to him. "Uh, yeah. It could be. We're supposed to do her in, right?"

"Then get to shootin'," his companion exclaimed.

The first bullet spanged off the brass-chased shaft of the handsome trotter that pulled Philipe's carriage. The second smacked into the dashboard and cracked its highly laquered inner surface. Immediately, Lone Wolf and Rebecca returned fire.

"I didn't see them," Philipe shouted, trying to

control the frightened, slightly wounded horse.

"Over there in the shadows. At the doorway," Rebecca told him, pointing it out with another round from her .44 Smith American.

A groan sounded loud after the report and a man's body toppled forward, face-first in the slime-running gutter. A second figure bolted from the insecure hiding place and Lone Wolf led him a moment before his Remington spoke and the fleeing gunman attempted to practice unpowered flight, his heels rising as his upper torso slammed forward under the force of the slug.

"Tulley must have sent men out to hunt for us," Rebecca observed.

"Which makes our job not any easier," Philipe opined.

"We are too vulnerable in this coach," Rebecca suggested. "We'd better park it somewhere and go on foot. That way we can watch both sides of the street, ahead and behind."

"Good idea," Lone Wolf declared.

Philipe mastered his panicked horse and trotted it to a pipe and chain tie-rail at the corner of Canal and Rampart. The trio climbed from the sturdy Studebaker and started down Canal toward the docks.

As they neared Bourbon, a voice called from a balcony, "There they are!"

Three shots blasted into the stillness. In the distance, a policeman's tin whistle could be heard tweeting.

Rebecca took aim into the midst of the muzzle blasts and fired two fast shots.

"Goddamn, I'm hit!" a rough voice bellowed.

All three would-be targets fired this time. A man screamed and staggered into view and the original wounded man managed only a stifled groan before his body hit the cobbles.

"Turn down Bourbon," Philipe suggested. "We'll go to St. Peter and then right to Jackson Square."

Footsteps tracked the trio down Bourbon Street. To add to their peril, Rebecca caught a fleeting glance of hurried movement in the small courtyard of the Absinth House.

"Down!" she shouted an instant before two six-guns blazed and bullets knocked plaster from the face of the building beyond them. She and Lone Wolf returned the fire to no effect and they sprinted on down the street. Near the intersection of Toulouse, where a single, dim street lamp glowed, Rebecca saw a familiar figure crouched on an overhanging balcony. She signaled her companions to stop and they faded into heavy shadow.

"Across the street over there," she whispered. "That's Owen Prather squatting down on the balcony. Wherever he is, Luke Wellington won't be far away. Lone Wolf, ah, Bret, backtrack to the last side street and come around on his blind side."

Lone Wolf nodded and trotted away. Less than a minute passed before startled voices came from the direction he had taken.

"What the hell . . . ?"

"It's one of them."

Shots ripped through the night.

Jake Tulley heard the gunfire, closer now, and

ached to be in on the kill. Roger Styles had ordered him to remain with him, though. Every man they had, including the reliable Luke Wellington, had been sent into the streets. They had to be able to stop that blasted girl and whoever she had with her.

"I don't like the sound of that," Roger remarked, while he poured himself a generous three fingers of brandy. "I think it would be a good time to visit Captain Decker."

The suggestion amazed Jake. "You mean run away? We've got eleven men out there."

"Considerably less, I would judge from the nearness of those shots."

"Maybe the boys got 'em the last time."

"We can't gamble on that, Jake. No, I feel we should leave here and head for the docks. The important thing is that you and I get away from this and start over somewhere else. I want to even things with her as much as you do, only . . ." the suave, handsome master criminal paused. He ran long, tapered fingers through his wavy black hair, then polished off the last of his brandy. "Revenge is a luxury we can ill afford at this point. We'll travel light, only what is packed in our bags. We can have the hotel's boy bring the rest behind us."

"I don't like it," Jake grumbled. "Runnin' away from a slip of a girl."

"Who has, let me remind you, damned near exterminated your entire gang, ruined two carefully developed plans of mine and shot to death one of her own uncles. That is no mere 'slip of a girl.' "

"You're afraid of her," Jake exploded, astonished at the possibility.

"Not . . . afraid, exactly. It's only that she has turned out to be more of a threat than could be expected from a young woman. The western territories are vast. We can settle in some place where she'll never know we're operating. I have already sent a telegram to Ezekial Caldwell. I told him to meet us in Austin, Texas. From there we can find the place with the proper climate for our activities to prosper. Believe me, Jake, it's the only way."

Rebecca felt a small clutch of anxiety. Their pursuers had not come any closer, which must mean that Lone Wolf had finished them off. But . . . had they, in turn, killed him? The minutes ran by in continued silence.

Then she saw a slight movement below the balcony across the street.

"Owen," a familiar voice called softly.

Owen Prather rose and leaned over the wrought iron rail.

Rebecca and Lone Wolf fired at the same time.

Two slugs burnt into Prather's flesh. Lone Wolf's, from below, hit high in his chest and straightened him up. He tried to scream, but could not. Blood and bone chips filled the airway from his lungs.

Rebecca's bullet drilled through the right side of his chest, deflected downward and brought ruin to a liver already damaged from excessive drinking. Owen Prather swayed momentarily, then did a header over the railing and landed with a wet smack on the brick pavement of Bourbon Street.

"Only another block to go," Philipe gusted out in a breath he suddenly realized he'd been holding far too long.

"Let's hurry," Rebecca advised.

With the young, vengeance-hungry white squaw in the lead, they rounded the corner into St. Peter Street. A fraction of a second later, Rebecca rebounded off the broad chest of Luke Wellington.

"Be damned!" he exploded and pinioned her arms. Then Lone Wolf and Philipe reached the struggling pair.

Philipe's foot smacked into the side of the gunhawk's head and he released his grip on Rebecca's arms and staggered back. Before anyone could fire a shot or close with the outlaw, he spun on one heel and ran away from them toward the dark mouth of an alley.

Rebecca sprinted ahead of the others, her .44 American leading the way.

At the entranceway to the cluttered alley, she paused and listened for retreating footsteps. None could be heard. Wellington had to be hiding in ambush. Crouched low, she cautiously advanced.

A sudden rustle and clatter of refuse brought a quick shot from the .44. A stray cat yowled in protest and disappeared from sight. Rebecca silently chided herself for reacting too quickly. Then she considered the dangerous situation she had entered into and decided she couldn't do otherwise. Rats scurried and squeaked a few inches ahead of her feet as she continued along the slimy passageway.

Rebecca took advantage of every crate, barrel or

mound of mouldering garbage, eyes strained to see in the pervasive gloom. Without warning, a box hurtled down at her from a wrought-iron stairway. At the last instant her senses perceived it and she leaped aside and fired a shot upward.

Even while the slug spanged off metal grillework, she snapped open the tilt-top revolver and ejected spent cartridges. From a pouch at her waist she extracted six fresh rounds and quickly reloaded. Another small crate plummeted down to smash to bits on the hard surface of the alley. Rebecca stepped into the center of the open space and aimed upward.

Three closely spaced bullets brought a rewarding groan. A second later, a Colt revolver clattered down the iron treads and pitched over the side. Rebecca sought the foot of the staircase.

Crouched low to present less target, Rebecca climbed the creaking steps, revolver cocked and ready. On the first grate-covered landing she saw a dark form huddled in a tight ball. Cautiously she moved forward.

"You caught me a right good one," Luke Wellington groaned.

"If you expect any help, tell me where to find Roger Styles and Jake Tulley."

A gasp escaped the gunman's pale lips and he continued to press both hands tightly over the bullet hole in his lower abdomen. "Th-the Hotel Le Provencial. O-on Jackson Square."

"How did they plan to send the girls out of here?"

"Aaah. Oh, God, this hurts. They w-were using a ship."

"What one?"

Wellington groaned again and made an effort to shrug. "Ah, what difference does it make? The *Moroney*. It's tied up at a dock on the other side of the French Market."

"Thank you, Luke," Rebecca told him in a gentle tone. Slowly she brought up the muzzle of the .44 American. "Now, since you were along when Jake Tulley sent me into five years of hell, I'm going to give you some help. You'd die from that gunshot if I left you here. So, I'm going to send you on to the real hell."

Her finger tightened on the trigger, the hammer fell and Luke Wellington died with a scream on his lips.

When Rebecca rejoined Philipe and Lone Wolf, they started immediately for Jackson Square. When they reached the Cathedral side of the immense garden spot, a cannon exploded a short distance away.

"The White League," Philipe exclaimed and added a curse.

Rifles and pistols crackled around the square. Across from them, near the high wall of the Saint Louis Hotel, now converted to the state capitol building, black faces could be made out in the dim light, defending the home of their "black-and-tan" Legislature from behind cotton bales. Both sides had small field pieces, inexpertly manned, which blasted away from time to time.

"Those fools are going to cause more trouble and grief for everyone," Philipe said in a tight voice as the trio sheltered behind the thick, protective wall of the Cathedral. "They say they want to unseat the carpetbaggers and run the rump Legislature out of office. Riots are not the way to accomplish that."

More shots rattled from the square and the cannons fired again. The clatter of many hoofs could be heard in the distance.

"That'll be the army coming," Philipe observed. "We'll have to run for our lives. Any white person caught out here will be fair game for the troops."

"But what about Styles and Tulley?" Rebecca protested. "Their hotel is right over there."

"The darkies are using grapeshot. You wouldn't last past that lamp post," Philipe told her. "I wonder why the lights weren't shot out the first thing?"

"The attackers needed them to see, same as the ones behind the bales," Lone Wolf observed.

"This could go on for a long time. Let's hurry away," Philipe urged.

Regretfully, Rebecca turned her back on the hotel where her arch-enemies could be cornered and followed Philipe back to the next intersection, at Royal Street.

"We might as well go to the wharf," Rebecca suggested. Hoof beats grew louder and they drew back into teh darkness of a tunnel-like recessed entryway.

Mounted soldiers clattered past, sabres agleam in the scant light of street lamps. Shouts of alarm rose from Jackson Square and members of the White League began a hasty retreat.

"There'll be more of that, I'm afraid," Philipe remarked.

"While they're at it," Rebecca urged, "let's get Styles and Tulley."

CHAPTER 18

A few scattered shots and screams still came from Jackson Square ten minutes later while Rebecca and her companions squatted in hiding behind a stack of boxes and bales of coffee beans outside the quayside entrance of the French Market. Rich odors of spices, vanilla beans and other rare commodities filled the air. They had located the *Moroney* easily and now kept constant watch. Three figures appeared at the stern rail and Rebecca recognized the stout figure and bowler hat of Jake Tulley.

"There they are. We could shoot them from here," Rebecca remarked excitedly.

"Two men without even a weapon in sight?" Philipe countered her. "Thanks to the White League, the Quarter is swarming with police and troops. If we fired a shot right now, they would fall on us in a second. Chances are we'd wind up being hanged for murder."

"Any idea what we can do?"

"Wait. The riot will be quelled by daylight. Meanwhile we can work out some way to get on board without you two being recognized."

"Not an easy task," Lone Wolf offered.

"There has to be a way," Rebecca declared with fierce determination.

Shortly after sunrise, preparations began for getting the *Moroney* under way. Men scurried around the deck freeing hawsers and making ready to hoist sail. A messenger boy, wearing a dark blue jacket and a flat-topped bill cap of the same color walked onto the wharf and yelled up to the deck that he had been sent over by the hotel clerk to locate a Mister Roger Styles. The deckhand he hailed conferred with his watch chief, who called the lad aboard the ship. He was shown to a main deck cabin into which Styles and Tulley had disappeared an hour before.

"Telegram for Mr. Roger Styles," the lad announced in a high, piping voice.

"Thank you, boy," Roger replied, taking the yellow message form and handing the youngster a silver dime.

The child's eyes widened at the generous size of the tip and he made hasty thanks before he dashed out the door. Roger opened the folded piece of paper and read the contents. As he did, he flushed an angry dark red.

"Here, read this," he snarled when he finished.

"Awh, Roger, you know I cain't read," Jake Tulley protested.

"I'll do it for you. 'Be advised that the cargo you expected from the west will not be arriving. It was stopped in Arkansas by a woman calling herself Rebecca Caldwell. Only two of us escaped a murderous night time attack by Indians, who worked in cahoots with her. Others killed between here and Kansas, those who survived scattered. All is lost here. Clive Dunkan.' Son of a bitch!" Roger burst out. He rarely used harsh language and his utterance now seemed all the more effective for it.

"Does that mean we have to give Captain Decker back his money?" Jake asked.

Roger looked thoughtfully at his underling. "Sometimes, Jake, I don't think you have both oars in the water. Hell, yes, we have to give the money back. Worse, we'll have to pay for passage to some other port. That infernal female has done more to harm us than an army of sheriffs and vigilance committees could ever manage. The time is overdue to turn the tables on her. We have to hunt her down, corner her and finish her once and for all."

"That's what the boys are doing now."

"Not with any great success."

"It's that damned riot, Roger," Jake offered.

A knock sounded and Captain Decker entered the cabin. "Two of your men here. They say they've got something important."

"Send them in," Roger requested, fearing the worst.

When they entered, the gunslicks looked apprehensive and fidgeted with their hats, which they had removed. "Uh, Boss, Mr. Styles, you're not going to like this . . ." one began hesitantly.

"Get on with it," Jake growled.

"Well, we lost all track of the Caldwell girl in the riot last night. Seven of the boys got killed, eight countin' Luke Wellington."

"What! Luke dead?" Jake blurted. "How did it happen?"

"Don't know for sure. But he was shot up close. His face is black with powder marks and the whole back of his head is blowed off."

"That ties it all. You mean to tell me that outside of you two, there's only three men left?"

"Yes, sir," the gunhand told Roger.

"A bunch of the boys are with Ezekial," Jake offered hopefully.

"Only he's clear the hell off in Kansas somewhere, on his way to Texas. A lot of good they do us now."

"There's always Captain Decker's men."

"They're sailors, not gunhandlers."

"We'll be gone in a few hours," Jake suggested hesitantly. "Didn't Cap'n Decker say we'd sail on the evening tide?"

"Meanwhile, Rebecca Caldwell can come after us and we'll be lucky to stop her, let alone anyone with her. The way she's using up our men, I wouldn't doubt she could walk right in this cabin and gun us both down."

Workers and clerks arriving to open the French Market drove the trio from their observation place. "I'll stay here," Lone Wolf offered. In that little park over there where I can keep an eye on them in case they get off the ship. You two should get some rest."

"Where?" Phillipe inquired both hands out, palms up in a Gallic gesture. "The entire city is in a turmoil after last night's riot."

"We can go to my hotel," Rebecca offered. "It's

close by." The erotic gleam of anticipation in her eyes was matched by one in Philipe's.

"That's a good idea," Lone Wolf agreed. "I'll get word to you if Styles or Tulley try to leave."

They made it to the corner of Toulouse and Royal, two blocks from her hotel, when a shout raised among a cluster of muttering people across the street from them. "The bulls! The bulls are coming!" a boy yelled.

Immediately, the gathering began to scatter. Rebecca and Philipe failed to move in time. From three directions, running policemen, accompanied by horse-drawn paddy wagons converged on the intersection. They wielded billy clubs with indifferent abandon, striking the heads of men, women and children with equal force and suddenness. Behind the advancing police, others in their blue uniforms grabbed unconscious victims of the trouncings and dragged them to the open rear doors of the black marias. One small boy, with blood and yellow fluid seeping frm the split in his skull, cried out sharply, convulsed and died. Uncaring, the policeman pulling on his ankle shrugged, let go and went for another.

One nightstick swished through the air close to Rebecca and Philipe sheltered her. He spoke out with such force that it arrested the motion of the police officer who swung the club and two others.

"Stop this at once!" he demanded. "Watch what you're doing, fellow, or I'll have your badge."

The beefy, red-faced harness bull glowered at Philipe. His tone of command, quality of speech and clothing left no doubt that Philipe was of the upper class among New Orleans citizens. It gave cause for worry on the part of the brutal lawman.

"Who are you, Mister? And state your business on the street."

Philipe drew himself up to his most considerable height, gray eyes flashing and nostrils flared. "I am Philipe Edouard Raymond DuBois, the Third. As to my business, I have a perfect right on this street." Philipe waved a casual hand toward Royal. "I own half of this block. Not to mention Yellow Tree and Old Hickory plantations. I am also a whist partner of your chief of police. If you are incapable of recognizing your betters, my good man, I would advise you to be less liberal in the application of that nightstick."

The policeman gaped and stammered. At Philipe's side, Rebecca experienced equal astonishment. She knew Philipe to be comfortably situated, though she had no idea how wealthy he might be. Apparently he was quite a power to be reckoned with.

"Y-your pardon, sir. I . . . me an' my men will provide you and the lady an escort if you wish, Mr. DuBois. There's more trouble brewin' with these White Leaguers. The Governor an' Legislature are meetin' to declare martial law. Be best if we was to see you safe to your destination, sir."

"That won't be necessary, but thank you all the same. As to martial law, those performing monkeys of the Carpetbaggers' will do as the whim strikes them. If they had half a brain among them, they would exert their lazy, shiftless hides to root out the corruption in government, and thus present no excuse for the excesses of the White League. It's that or see the ranks of the mob increased a hundred fold. Now, if you will excuse us, we'll be on our way."

Once past the policemen, Rebecca spoke in a small,

strained voice. "Philipe? I . . . I had no idea you were so influential in local affairs."

The handsome descendant of French nobility smiled gently at her. "Does it make any difference?"

"No. Only . . . now we can, *you* can impose on the authorities to hold that ship and haul Roger Styles and Jake Tulley off to face justice."

"Court justice, or your own brand?"

Rebecca's hopeful expression faded. She knew in her heart that she wanted a part in doing in Jake Tulley for his perfidy and Roger Styles for raping her. Courts of law did not figure in her plan.

By the time they reached the Maison Du Prix, Rebecca's spirits had been restored. She had no sooner closed the door to her room than she began to undress. Philipe quickly caught up to her and they stood nude by the bedside, embracing and kissing deeply. She felt the heat of his loins and the sudden surge of his thick phallus. They stepped apart and she climbed on the bed on all fours.

"Take me from behind," she urged, then shivered with delight as his hot, turbid lance nestled between the cleft of her buttocks and sought the gaping, wet opening to her treasure trove. She grunted with pleasure as he found his goal and gave a mighty thrust that expanded her orifice to the maximum of its ability to stretch. In this position, the sensitive bottom surface of the fiery member ran repeatedly over that small bean of absolute rapture that was cushioned in the upper arch of her channel.

Surch friendly friction heightened the sensations of joy for both of them. Over and over, as Philipe drove his bulging manhood into her pulsing purse, mighty jolts of pure ecstasy raced through her body, drawing cries of happiness from far inside her, sapping all her strength, only to have it renewed for still more onslaughts of magical delirium. Gradually her straining partner rose up the pinnacle and burst into completion along with her final, gasping release.

Twice more they made furious, ennervating love before they lay side by side and rested from their magnificent endeavors.

"There's not another man in the world who loves so completely, Philipe."

"Oh? Have you tried them all?"

"No, you ox!" Rebecca cried. "It's just how I feel after we've . . . been together. Sometimes I'm afraid you will split me wide open. Others, I'm sorry you don't. What a way to go—shattered with joy."

"You are being fanciful."

"I'm trying to tell you how it is for me. Women are not expected to like or take pleasure from sex. At least that was what I had been taught as a small girl. Then I made love with an Oglala boy, Two Horny, who later became my husband. It made me sick." She paused and Philipe looked at her quizzically. "Sick at heart that I had wasted all those years until sixteen during which I could have been enjoying that wonderful thing to my heart's content as often as I could." Rebecca started to giggle and Philipe's baritone laughter joined her.

He broke off to cover her pert, upthrust breasts with kisses. She reached for his penis and found it already rigid. She squeezed it and began to slowly stroke. Philipe's caresses and smacking lips grew more fervent and she caught at her breath. Instantly she guided his throbbing shaft to the warmth and moisture of her eager, ever-ready cavern.

An hour later, Lone Wolf knocked at the door. Hurriedly they threw on clothes and Rebecca admitted her friend.

"The ship is sailing," he announced.

"What! We have to go after it," Rebecca exclaimed. "Hurry, let's do something to stop them."

"It's this riot situation," Lone Wolf explained. "Someone in charge at the docks went to all ships that didn't have New Orleans for a home port and ordered them to sail, whether they had finished their business or not. At least down river to the delta until this is over. With fewer foreign sailors in the city, they expect to be able to put down the rioters."

"Oh, of all times for . . ." Rebecca caught herself. Never complain or show weakness, she told herself. A good Oglala is trained better than that.

"I have a friend with a speedy cutter . We can use that," Philipe suggested.

Rebecca clapped her hands together. "We can follow them down the river. Somehow we'll figure a way to get aboard."

Half an hour later, Philipe and two acquaintances crewed the swift sailboat as it left the dock and pointed its jib-boom northward, following the crescent of the Mississippi up past the *Vieux Carre* on the left bank and Algiers on the right. Heavy traffic slowed their pace for a while, until they rounded the point and started southeast away from the city.

Rebecca thought long and hard about a means of

boarding the *Moroney* without their identity being instantly discovered. The more she concentrated, the more elusive the answer became. She took to pacing the deck, eyes on the distant horizon of Spanish moss-haloed cypress and small, stunted brush. Though most often she kept her gaze on the shiny brown ribbon of the river. Up there, not far ahead of them, were the men she most wanted to kill.

"We have to get ahead of them." Sudden inspiration had hit her. "I have an idea. But we will have to go on by without attracting any attention."

"And then what?"

"Then we're going to have something . . . ah, happen to the boat. I don't know about ships and things, so you will have to figure that out, Philipe. Anyway we have to block the river in such a way they can't get past. Or call to them for help. Something."

"What says they will stop for us?" Lone Wolf inquired.

"Nobody is *all* bad," Rebecca returned. "The captain will have to do something about it."

"That is correct," Philipe added. "My business interests have made me most familiar with maritime law. If we show some distress signal, the captain will have no choice but to offer aid."

"Then we get on board. You and I will have to change our features somehow, Lone Wolf."

"That's twice you've called Bret by that name. I don't want to be rude, but what is its significance?"

"I lived with the Crow for ten years, Philipe," Lone Wolf told him. "That was the name they gave me when I accepted their ways and became a warrior. Somehow, after the raid on Rebecca's Sioux village when we escaped together, I never got back to calling myself Bret Baylor. For some reason, it doesn't seem to fit me any more. So, I go by Lone Wolf and that does me well enough."

"Unusual among whites, isn't it?"

"I try to, ah, avoid them as much as possible, Philipe."

"Except for Jake Tulley and his gang?"

"A point for you. Now," he returned to the original subject. "What are the two of us going to do against the ship's crew, Tulley and whoever else is along with him?"

"Three of us," Philipe inserted.

"The, uh, three of us will go for Tulley and his gang and Roger Styles. The men on that ship won't be loyal to Roger or to Jake. Like bystanders in a town, I'm willing to bet they will stay out of the way when the shooting starts. The important thing is fooling the captain enough to get us on board. Then we have Roger and Jake trapped. It's only a matter of hunting them down on the ship and . . . eliminating them."

CHAPTER 19

By mid-afternoon those on board the speedy cutter caught sight of the high stern of the *Moroney*. All about them the low, swamp and marsh land seemed almost indistinguishable from the mighty mud-tinted river they sailed upon. By then, the details had been worked out on the nature of the "emergency."

There would be a "fire" and some "injured people." Three of them. Two so badly mangled they would be swathed in bandages, Rebecca and Lone Wolf, the third, Philipe, ambulatory. Accordingly, when the trim craft sped past the slower moving steam vessel, the young woman and her companion remained below decks, out of sight. The *Marie Jeaneu* would proceed over the horizon from the freighter, then stage the accident.

"We don't know how many of the crew are in on this child-stealing scheme," Lone Wolf told Rebecca while they sat on low bunks opposite each other. "I don't share your confidence that the men on board will stand aside and let us deal with Styles and Tulley."

"I suppose it's good for one of us to remain doubtful," Rebecca allowed. "We'll know soon enough, once we get on board. Tulley has five men with him. Where they'll be I don't know."

"Not in the same cabin with Roger Styles. That would be beneath his dignity."

"You're right about that. Probably down inside the ship somewhere."

"Not likely in the holds, though maybe in the crew's quarters," Lone Wolf speculated.

"If that's the case, we may have finished Styles and Tulley before any of them realize what's happened."

"With a lot of luck, yes."

Philipe's head appeared in the rectangular opening to the companionway. "You two had better start getting done up to be victims."

"So soon?"

"We've outdistanced them by about an hour. That should be plenty of time to make our charade believable."

From a hanging locker, Philipe took a large roll of gauze and some tape. Rebecca swathed Lone Wolf's face in bandages, providing open space only for eyes, nose and mouth. She arranged his left arm so that the sling concealed a steel-headed tomahawk which he could wield unencumbered by the wrappings on his hand. Next, Philipe smeared Lone Wolf's clothes with soot made from burned corks. With the help of Ron Girrard, the *Marie Jeaneu's* owner, Philipe then made similar adornments for Rebecca.

In her bandaged right fist, appearing like nothing more than an extended index finger and thumb, she held her Baby Russian. Lastly, Philipe added touches to his own appearance to complete the ruse. He wrinkled his nose at the offensive odor of burned hair when he singed his long brown locks with the flame of a small lamp. As an after thought, he scorched some of Rebecca's hair and that of Lone Wolf, to give them a properly burned smell.

"Now," Philipe mumbled through the bandage that covered part of his jaw and mouth, "we're ready to have a disastrous fire below decks."

Jake Tulley paced the restricted area of the small cabin like a caged animal. "I don't like this, closed up places like this. Makes me think of jail cells."

"Something you're well enough familiar with, I dare say," Roger replied sarcastically. "Pour some brandy and relax. We're safe enough now."

"Where is Rebecca Caldwell? She didn't simply give up. She's out there somewhere, after us. I can sense it."

"If you are going to continue that infernal pacing, please do so out on deck," Roger demanded.

A knock sounded and Jake opened the door to reveal the First Officer of the *Moroney*, Harold Godfrey. Although round of head and face, he had a ferret quality to his features and cupped ears that stood out from his greasy blond locks. His eyes were of that particular pale blue that made it appear he looked through, rather than at, a person. He had an almost simpering smile that irritated both Roger and Jake on sight. His voice was soft, vaguely effeminate.

"The Captain's compliments, gentlemen. He'd like you to join him for dinner tonight."

"How very sweet," Jake growled.

Roger's better breeding won through. "We'd be delighted. Give the Captain our thanks. What time?"

"Three bells of the mid-watch. For landlubbers that would be seven this evening. No need for formal attire."

"We'll be there."

After Mister Godfrey had departed, Roger smashed one fist into his palm. "Decker probably wants to hold us up for more money. Why else would he invite us to dinner?"

"Yeah," Jake returned in a surly tone. "I think I will go out on deck. That pursed-lipped little shit stunk up the air in here."

On the broad foredeck of the *Moroney*, Jake found the sweet-sour stench of the sloughs more pronounced in the stiff breeze that howled through the bare rigging. To facilitate steering, only courses and top gallant sails had been shaken out and it left many reeved lines, each to sound its mournful tune. Five men left, Jake thought with trepidation. At least until the others could be rounded up and arrive in Texas. Decker had one more stop, at Galveston, before setting sail for the Mediterranean. Texas suited Jake Tulley. He liked the idea. A big, unsettled place with plenty of opportunities to grab a fortune. Even if it belonged to someone else.

He paced along the weather rail, aimed for the bowsprit. It would be dark in another three hours. How sudden it came in these parts. In an instant he found himself missing the beautiful colors of the lingering sunsets of the prairie. All rose and purple and gold, with the softest line of blue dividing the fat ball of the sun and its display of rich colors from the black dome of night that spread from the east. A rueful smile came to his lips. God, that sounded almost like a poem. And he hated poetry . . . it was sissy. Still, a twinge of something Jake would not identify as homesickness made him long for the vast spaces of the western range. A smudge of smoke ahead of the big ship caught his attention.

As he peered forward, the slender masts of a fair-sized boat rose over the horizon, then the hull. Flags, which meant nothing to Jake, had been raised on a long, slanting line to the main mast. He heard a shout from above and behind him in the crow's nest and turned to see hurried activity on the quarterdeck. He glanced again at the source of the smoke and started for the cabin to tell Roger. Anything, at a time like this, seemed suspicious to Jake.

Fifteen minutes later, the big steam engines of the *Moroney* backed down and the great side-wheel paddles stopped thrashing. Captain Decker stood beside his uncommonly grim-faced second in command. As their former momentum carried them on the tide toward the cutter that lay athwart their beam, the captain raised a large leather hailing megaphone.

"Ahoy, the *Marie Jeaneu!* What is the nature of your emergency?"

"We've had a fire below decks," came Ron Girrard's answer. "And we have injured persons who need medical care at once. Do you have a doctor aboard?"

"Yes," Decker replied in a reluctant tone.

"Can you take our injured aboard then? At least as far as Port Sulphur to the hospital there?"

"Why . . . I . . ." Decker paused when Roger Styles hurried up to his side.

"What's goin on? Why are we stopping for that boat?"

"Maritime regulations. If we didn't stop to answer their call for assistance, they would report us and I'd lose my license."

"It could be a trick," Roger replied, anxiety sounding for the first time in his voice. Jake's suspicions had infected him.

"If you are concerned about that, I suggest you stay in your cabin, out of sight. The same for your men."

"I demand that . . ."

"No," Captain Decker growled. "On this ship, it is I who give the orders. Go to your cabin and keep your men below. Everything will be all right." He turned away to hail the distressed sailcraft.

Roger stomped across the quarterdeck and descended to the cabin deck.

"On the *Marie Jeaneu*. We will take your injured to Port Sulphur. Stand by for a cargo net to be rigged to sway them inboard."

"Thank you, Captain."

It took ten more minutes for the deck crew to rig a suitable platform to be operated by the cargo boom. They bent backs to the lines and swung the big brass-collared wooden beam out over the side. With one to act as rigger, the winch-pawl was released and the pallet lowered over the side. At a signal from the sailor leaning over the rail, the drum was reversed and the burden brought up.

A groaning figure, swathed in bandages and lashed to the platform came into view. Crewmen hastened to remove the accident victim from the boards so the procedure could be repeated. Another white wrapped bundle came over the rail two minutes later.

"There's one more," Ron Girrard's voice called from the unseen deck of the *Marie Jeaneu*.

The third injured man could at least fend for himself, the officers on the quarterdeck saw. He stepped lightly onto the deck of the *Moroney*. Then he gestured for the crewmen to come closer. When they did, he displayed a cocked and ready Colt .45 Peacemaker.

"River pirates," one seasoned sailor blurted out.

"We did not come to take your ship, *mes amis*," Philipe informed them. "We are here after two passengers and the men with them. Kindly inform us where we can locate Roger Styles and Jake Tulley."

"We don't know any names. There's two dandies in Cabin B. Are they the ones you want?"

"Most likely. What about the men with them?"

"They're down below."

"Good. You would be wise to keep them there."

The other "victims" had sat up now and menaced the unarmed sailors with weapons of their own.

On the quarterdeck, First Officer Godfrey was first to suspect something had gone wrong. The deck hands stood around the supposedly injured man, whose back was to Godfrey, though none moved to aid any of the casualties. By now they should have had the new arrivals on the way to a cabin to be examined by the ship's doctor. He armed himself with a cutlass from the rack on the taff rail, to augment his revolver, and spoke to the captain.

"I think Styles may have been correct about a trap. There's something, ah, not quite right about those people. I'll go have a look."

"Yes," Decker said absently, more absorbed in the handling of the *Marie Jeaneu* so it would not come afoul of his own vessel. "You do that."

Godfrey descended the short flight of steps between the quarterdeck and the main deck and started forward at a fast pace. Still seated on the steel plates across from Philipe, Rebecca saw Godfrey coming, and the weapons he carried. She shouted a warning.

"Behind you, Philipe!"

Philipe DuBois leaped to one side and started to turn to face the unknown danger. As he did, Rebecca fired through her bandage. Smoke and smouldering bits of gauze bandage engulfed her hand. The .38 slug punched through the minor obstruction with ease, its trajectory and velocity little impaired.

Rebecca's first bullet struck Godfrey low on his left side.

He stumbled and winced with pain, then advancing, limping, with his gunhand pressed tightly against the wound. A wild light burned in his pale eyes. "I'll kill you for that," he grunted out.

Rebecca struggled in the confines of the bandage to recock her Smith Baby Russian. At last she maneuvered her thumb into the proper position and pulled backward. It caught for a fleeting moment, then ratcheted to full-cock. She fired again as he took a final step forward and swung the cutlass at Philipe DuBois.

The keen edge bit into flesh near the point of Philipe's shoulder an instant before Rebecca's second bullet shattered Godfrey's wrist, directly behind the hilt of the sword. He screamed and let go, glancing at the sailors who, being unarmed, jumped backward, out of the line of fire, the moment the first shot had gone off.

"Get them, men!" Godfrey commanded.

None of the crewmen moved while Lone Wolf's tomahawk whistled through the air and buried its sharp edge to the haft in Godfrey's forehead. The Fire Officer of the *Moroney* went to the deck like a pole-axed steer. Immediately, Rebecca came to her feet and the three attackers made a dash for the cabin deck. Only three seamen trailed after them.

"What the hell's going on out there?" Roger demanded at the sound of a shot.

"I can't tell," Jake replied. "There ain't no windows on this side."

"Portholes," Roger corrected. "Open the door and take a look.

"You crazy? I knew somethin' was wrong. It has to be that damned Caldwell girl."

Another shot sounded, followed by a shriek of pain.

"Shit. They'll be comin' here next," Jake bemoaned. "We're trapped."

"Then let's get out of here. Go below with the men."

Jake needed no extra prodding to agree with that idea. He flung open the door and ran along the semi-open gangway toward a ladder that led into the bowels of the ship. Roger pounded along at his heels.

Behind him, Jake heard the approach of several pair of footsteps. He drew his Colt and turned at the waist. Roger veered to the side and kept on running while Jake cocked his weapon and threw a hurried shot in back of them, toward the bow of the ship.

Philipe's Colt, Lone Wolf's Remington and Rebecca's Baby Russian answered him. Lead slugs screamed off the hardwood paneling of the passage. One put a crease along Roger's ribs. He grunted with pain and sprinted the last few feet to the open hatchway. Jake fired three more, measured shots, then dived down the open companionway.

"That's where the rest of the gang will be," Rebecca cautioned. "We'd better stop here. I've got to get these burning bandages off my hand and free the other one to use the .44. And, Philipe, we'll have to stop the bleeding in that wound."

"I am about useless, *mon cher*. The cutlass went quite deep." Blood ran in a torrent from the cut in Philipe's shoulder. Rebecca quickly removed the gauze from her hand and used the clean parts to form a pad. The long strips Lone Wolf removed from her head would serve as a bandage. She put the folded cloth in place over the large slash and began to wind the remainder over and around the cut.

"Hold it right there, you three," a growling voice declared behind them.

Three sailors stood blocking the gangway. One

hefted a boat hook, the others had obtained cutlasses. With ominous determination, they closed in.

Lone Wolf shot the first one in the head.

Blood, fluid and brain matter sprayed from the exit wound on the right side of the sailor's skull. His mates leaped forward in a mad rush.

Rebecca raised her .44 Smith American in her left hand and punched a hole in the abdomen of the man with the boat hook. He staggered forward on rubbery legs, while a wet smear of blood spread from the black hole an inch above his navel.

Behind it, the hot bullet had torn through his intestines and clipped one lobe off his liver. He died before he hit the deck.

Immediately, Rebecca centered on the last target. The man threw down his cutlass and started to run. She took careful aim and cut his left leg out from under him with a slug in his thigh. With a cry of pain he sprawled on the steel plates of the foredeck.

Bullets howled off the metal overhead and caused the trio of avengers to duck. Tulley's men had nerved themselves to enter the fight. Rebecca reasoned that Philipe had to be the weakest one in her party.

"Philipe, watch our backs for any more sailors who want to take a hand. We'll move in on Tulley and the others."

Rebecca quickly emptied the big .44 and snapped it open to reload. With six fresh cartridges in place, she locked the cylinder and barrel assembly in place and fired twice more into the dark opening that led below. She made a mental note that she had only nine rounds remaining in her belt pouch. A face appeared in the hatchway and she cranked off a shot.

A thin spray of blood and bone flashed in the air where the face had been. Then more wild shots blasted out to spread gray smears on the steel plates of the overhead. Lone Wolf darted beyond the companionway to provide another angle of fire. Swiftly, Rebecca moved closer.

Another brave gunhawk poked his head and a Colt-filled hand over the transom. He caught a bullet from both directions. The hot lead bulged his eyes and heaved him partly upright. Then he sunk into the slack posture of death. Running feet, instead of gunshots, sounded from the lower deck. Rebecca reached the hatchway first.

Cautiously she poked one eye beyond the frame. No fire answered her. She saw a dimly lighted corridor at the bottom of a slightly angled iron rung ladder. A body lay crumpled at the base. Not a sign of Styles, Tulley or their men. She motioned to Lone Wolf.

"Come on. We'll have to hunt them out."

Unfamiliar with the interior of the big ship, Tulley and his gunslingers soon got lost. They clattered up and down ladders until two of the remaining three found themselves in the engine room.

"How do we get out of here?" they demanded of the black gang.

"The way you came in."

"I mean to get out to the open."

"That ladder over there," the chief engineer pointed. "Straight up three decks."

The two outlaws clambered up the metal rungs with the speed of monkeys.

Jake Tulley had stayed close to Roger Styles during their flight. He stood panting now in a storage locker, filled with food for the impending voyage. Carefully, Roger eased the hatch closed and turned the handle to lock it in place.

"They can't get through that," he informed Jake. Then he pressed a fine quality linen handkerchief to the bullet graze on his side, muttering curses at Rebecca Caldwell.

"Yeah. But they're still out there."

"Captain Decker won't let them run around his ship shooting at people for long," Roger promised. "Now be quiet. They might hear us."

Footsteps sounded dully on the deck plates outside the compartment. The clatter stopped and an unseen person tried the battened hatch.

"Do you think they could be in there?" a feminine voice inquired.

"Could be. But there might be several reasons why it has been locked. We'll keep looking and come back."

"That was them," Jake whispered after the steps moved on. "We could get 'em easy."

"I still think they were behind that closed door," Rebecca insisted as they climbed again to the cabin deck level.

"I think it's called a hatch. There are so many places they could be. We've only searched half of the

211

ship and there's a limit to how much that captain is going to put up with. We killed one of his officers and he is in collusion with Styles and Tulley."

They turned a corner in the corridor which put them back where they had started. The long gangway was empty. Philipe DuBois no longer sat on guard at their rear. Rebecca hastened forward, Lone Wolf not far behind.

When they came out onto the foredeck, a belaying pin whirred through the air and struck Lone Wolf between the shoulder blades. He staggered forward and went to his knees, sharp pain radiating out from a pair of broken ribs.

"Grab her!" Captain Decker shouted.

Burly men swarmed over Rebecca before she could get off a shot. She kicked and struggled and tried to make use of her .44, all to no avail. The powerful sailors manhandled her across the deck to the rail and cast her overboard into the water. Lone Wolf, observing this, made a fast dash and dived cleanly over the side.

Hot tongues of agony lapped at him from the broken ribs and for a moment he could not orient himself. Then he saw Rebecca's dark head bobbing in the water. He reached Rebecca in five stout strokes. She seemed dazed slightly, barely able to tread water. Tears began to flood from her eyes.

"Are you all right?" he asked anxiously.

"Yes. Oh . . . no, *damnit*, I'm not. It's . . . it's that they're getting away again, damn their awful luck! There they go on that ship. And . . . and we can't do a thing about it."

She paused and dug an angry fist at the hot moisture streaming from her eyes. "And poor Philipe. If they didn't throw him overboard too, he's still on the ship and badly wounded."

CHAPTER 20

Ron Girrard's *Marie Jeaneu* had waited nearby during the furious activity aboard the *Moroney*. The competent young businessman and amateur sailor heard the shouts from Rebecca and Lone Wolf and picked them up. He had been close enough, in the fading light of late afternoon to see them tossed overboard.

"No," he replied in answer to their questions about Philipe being tossed over the side. "I would have seen it if that had been the case. He is, I am afraid, still aboard."

"Then we must follow. Styles and Tulley are capable of killing him out of hand. We can't let that happen," Rebecca appealed.

Girrard shrugged. "Short of a broadside of cannon, how do you propose to make them stop and deliver Philipe to us?"

"I . . . oh, I don't have any idea. I only know that we must keep that ship in sight."

Slowly the high stern of the *Moroney* moved serenely into the distance. Girrard hoisted all sail and they continued on down the river. Rebecca and Lone Wolf changed into dry clothing, while the cutter closed to a safe distance behind the ship bearing Styles and Tulley away from justice.

"I lost both revolvers," she announced suddenly.

"You can buy more in New Orleans," Lone Wolf told her.

Darkness came on them before the *Marie Jeaneu* reached the mouth of the Mississippi River. Obedient to the rules of the sea, Captain Decker lit all of his navigational lights and a white one to stern and at the mainmast top. It made following easy. Rebecca seethed at the inactivity. Like Lone Wolf, she felt a strong sense of failure. Worse, she had lost her weapons. Fortunately the mate to the lost .44 remained aboard the cutter. If only she could get another chance at Roger Styles and Jake Tulley.

"The *Moroney* just threw something over the side," Ron Girrard announced to them as they neared land's end at the river's mouth. "Bearing west-southwest. We can close with it in a few minutes."

"Could it be Philipe?" Rebecca asked excitedly, worry growing in her with each passing second.

"We'll soon know."

To Rebecca, who stood at the bow, peering anxiously into the dark waters, the minutes dragged by in reverse. Then Albert, the other friend of Philipe's who had come along, let out a shout from the port side of the boat.

"There! In the water. It looks like a person floating on his back. Hard aport!"

Rebecca rushed to stand beside him. "Is it . . . is it, Philipe?"

"I'm not sure. We can hope, *Mademoiselle* Caldwell."

When the floating object grew closer, Rebecca could not see well enough to be sure. She lived on hope. Beside her, Albert leaned far out.

"There. Got it with a boat hook. My . . . my God, it is Philipe!"

More dead than alive, Philipe DuBois was dragged aboard the *Marie Jeaneu* and carried below to a bunk. Despite her anxiety, Rebecca had to settle for sitting in the corner while Girrard and his friend, wise in the ways of the sea, worked on Philipe.

They pressed on his chest and forced a quantity of sea water from his lungs. Then again. He coughed and sputtered and tried feebly to move.

"Lie back, *mon ami*," Girrard commanded in a soft voice. "You are among friends and safe. Here, roll over and let us try that one more time."

Gagging and retching, Philipe gave up more salt water until his friends thought him out of danger. He tried to sit up, only to be pressed down again. Then Rebecca saw the raw, blistered circles where someone had applied a burning cigar tip to his flesh. He had a bullet wound in his thigh as well. Blood seeped from the cutlass slash and her makeshift bandage had been removed.

"We must return to New Orleans with all speed," Girrard declared. "It is imperative he be put into the hospital."

"Nonsense, old friend. I . . . feel . . . fin . . ." Philipe passed out in midsentence.

A week crawled by while Philipe slowly mended in

the hospital. Rebecca returned from visiting him one afternoon to find a message in her hotel box. Curious, she carried it to Lone Wolf's room before opening it.

The letter had been sent by one of Philipe's factors in Galveston. The *Moroney* had docked there, right enough, it said.

"Two gentlemen, fitting the descriptions given, left the ship," the letter went on. "They immediately hired horses and left town. My inquiries determined that their destination was Austin, the state capital. Beyond that we could learn no more. Please express my concern to my employer for his speedy recovery." It had been signed by Jacques le Boite.

"We know where Tulley has gone," Rebecca said quietly after reading the letter through a second time. "Somehow, though, I don't want to start after him so suddenly."

"You've fallen in love, Rebecca."

"No! I haven't time for all . . . Uh, yes. I have. I shouldn't have allowed it, but it's true. I can't leave Philipe until he is at least out of danger. I ran off from Matt Peterson like that. I won't do it again."

True to her determination, Rebecca spent the next two weeks visiting and cheering Philipe until the doctor pronounced him strong enough to be entirely out of danger. He would be leaving the hospital in two days. During those fourteen days, she had also straightened out her thinking.

It would not do to allow more precious days to slide past in which Jake Tulley could disappear entirely, leaving her deprived of revenge. She had a lot more to get even for now. Philipe had lost twenty-five pounds, weight he could not afford to see gone. His left arm would remain impaired slightly. He, like so many others, had paid a price for Rebecca's war. At least, she reasoned, she would see Philipe once more before she and Lone Wolf headed for Texas.

"Ah, there is the brightness of my life," Philipe exclaimed when Rebecca entered his room. He sat up, propped by three pillows, and read from a slim, leather-bound volume of verse.

Rebecca went to his side and kissed him lightly on the lips. "You look so much better. Nearly strong enough to . . ." she paused suggestively and let it hang. "Though I've come for something else."

"To at last say good-bye."

"Y—yes. I . . . I didn't want to be quite that abrupt, Philipe. Only, you're well now, or nearly so, and we know where Tulley went. At least in what part of Texas to start looking."

"Nothing can dissuade you from this mad quest?"

"No. At least not now when the end is so close in sight."

"Not . . . not even this?" Philipe inquired with a lurid twinkle. He reached out and caught her hand, pulled it under the covers and pressed it against his tumescent penis. Her eyes widened in surprised gladness.

"Oh, Philipe, you have recovered."

"Enough to want you desperately, my love."

"A-and I you."

Rebecca broke away, all thoughts of the chase fled from her mind. Hastily she undid the long row of buttons on the front of her full dress and pulled it free of her body. In no time she had her underthings off and stood naked beside Philipe's bed. With his help, she drew aside the covers and exposed his magnificent manhood.

It glistened and quivered with eagerness. With the healing of his wounds, his sap had returned. Rebecca reached for it and, as before, closed both hands around its immense girth. Slowly, lovingly she began to stroke.

"It has been much too long, my dear," Philipe advised her. "Much of that and things will happen too fast."

Rebecca climbed onto the bed then and straddled his supine frame, kness bent and extended up his sides. Again she circled his grand equipage and began to slaver it in the moistness created by her ready body. Slowly she lowered herself until she felt the pleasurable pain of his engorged phallus spreading wide her furnace-hot passage. Then, with wild abandon, she slammed down on it and a screech of pure delight accompanied the rendering of her walls as the throbbing shaft became buried in her burning canal.

Leaning forward, Rebecca rocked back and forth, teasing Philipe and gauging how closely she could bring him to an explosion before she eased off and let him subside. Her swaying breasts brushed his chest and sent shivers through his lean frame. She kissed the hard nipples of his breast and let her long braids swing and brush his flesh. Gradually her own passion rose and she increased the energy of her motion. It would be good . . . oh, so good.

Bells clamored in her head and she felt her own pinnacle approaching. Oh, so fond and fair a good-bye, she thought tenderly. She vowed to return, once her search had ended. Yes, return and have this magnificent moment forever. On she labored until she cried out in ecstasy and Philipe arched upward, driving deeply inside her to explode in a frenzy.

They lay side-by-side for a long while. Long shadows had fallen across the room from the open window. Outside the calls of children at play added to the romantic atmosphere. Rebecca reached for him again, kneading the flaccid flesh to new firmness. Philipe's dextrous fingers found her slippery opening and began to manipulate the delicate centers of excitement there. Long minutes passed in silent effort, mutually enjoyed, then Rebecca bent low and ran her tongue over the spongy, sensitive tip. Philipe writhed on his bed, though this time not from pain. On she worked, taking tiny fractions of an inch into her wide-spread mouth as she continued to spiral over the pulsating flesh that to her tasted so sweet and felt so silky. Neither of them heard the door open.

"Ow! Pardonez moi!" a flustered nurse exclaimed, then banged shut the portal.

Rebecca and Philipe began to chuckle. Their bout of guffaws and trills of laughter continued for fifteen minutes. All that while, she noticed, his wonderful member retained all its rigidity. Soon they sobered enough that Rebecca threw a leg over his hips and drew near, one hand guiding his fully charged weapon to its target.

By then, any memory of why she had come to say good-bye had left her.

THE NEWEST ADVENTURES AND ESCAPADES OF BOLT
by Cort Martin

#11: THE LAST BORDELLO (1224, $2.25)
A working girl in Angel's camp doesn't stand a chance—unless Jared Bolt takes up arms to bring a little peace to the town . . . and discovers that the trouble is caused by a woman who used to do the same!

#12: THE HANGTOWN HARLOTS (1274, $2.25)
When the miners come to town, the local girls are used to having wild parties, but events are turning ugly . . . and murderous. Jared Bolt knows the trade of tricking better than anyone, though, and is always the first to come to a lady in need . . .

#13: MONTANA MISTRESS (1316, $2.25)
Roland Cameron owns the local bank, the sheriff, and the town—and he thinks he owns the sensuous saloon singer, Charity, as well. But the moment Bolt and Charity eye each other there's fire—especially gunfire!

#14: VIRGINIA CITY VIRGIN (1360, $2.25)
When Katie's bawdy house holds a high stakes raffle, Bolt figures to take a chance. It's winner take all—and the prize is a budding nineteen year old virgin! But there's a passle of gun-toting folks who'd rather see Bolt in a coffin than in the virgin's bed!

#15: BORDELLO BACKSHOOTER (1411, $2.25)
Nobody has ever seen the face of curvaceous Cherry Bonner, the mysterious madam of the bawdiest bordello in Cheyenne. When Bolt keeps a pimp with big ideas and a terrible temper from having his way with Cherry, gunfire flares and a gambling man would bet on murder: Bolt's!

#16: HARDCASE HUSSY (1513, $2.25)
Traveling to set up his next bordello, Bolt is surrounded by six prime ladies of the evening. But just as Bolt is about to explore this lovely terrain, their stagecoach is ambushed by the murdering Beeler gang, bucking to be in Bolt's position!

Available wherever paperbacks are sold, or order direct from the Publisher. Send cover price plus 50¢ per copy for mailing and handling to Zebra Books, Dept. 1314, 475 Park Avenue South, New York, N.Y. 10016. DO NOT SEND CASH.

THE BEST IN HISTORICAL ROMANCE
by Elizabeth Fritch

TIDES OF RAPTURE (1245, $3.75)

When honey-haired Mandy encounters a handsome Yankee major, she's enchanted by the fires of passion in his eyes, bewitched by the stolen moments in his arms, and determined not to betray her loyalties! But this Yankee rogue has other things in mind!

CALIFORNIA, BOOK ONE: (1229, $3.50)
PASSION'S TRAIL

Before Sarah would give Toby her innocence, she was determined to make his destiny her own. And as they journeyed across the vast mountains and prairies, battling blizzards, drought and Indians, the two young lovers held the promise of riches and glory in their hearts — and the strength to shape a new frontier in the blazing, bountiful land of CALIFORNIA.

CALIFORNIA, BOOK TWO: (1309, $3.50)
GOLDEN FIRES

The passion Clint Rawlins stirred in Samantha's heart was wilder than the town he had come to tame. And though they fought against each other's independence and their own desires — they knew they were destined to share in the creation of the west, the lush, green land of California.

CALIFORNIA, BOOK THREE: (1439, $3.50)
A HEART DIVIDED

Awestruck by the wealth and power of the fabled Rawlins family in the San Francisco of 1906, Felicity was swept off her feet by the two Rawlins brothers. Unlike his upstanding brother Bryce, Hunt Rawlins thrived on the money, women, and danger of the Barbary Coast, but Felicity was drawn to him even though she realized his unscrupulous heart would never give her the lasting love offered by his brother.

Available wherever paperbacks are sold, or order direct from the Publisher. Send cover price plus 50¢ per copy for mailing and handling to Zebra Books, Dept. 1314, 475 Park Avenue South, New York, N.Y. 10016. DO NOT SEND CASH.

THE BESTSELLING ECSTASY SERIES
by Janelle Taylor

SAVAGE ECSTASY (824, $3.50)
It was like lightning striking, the first time the Indian brave Gray Eagle looked into the eyes of the beautiful young settler Alisha. And from the moment he saw her, he knew that he must possess her—and make her his slave!

DEFIANT ECSTASY (931, $3.50)
When Gray Eagle returned to Fort Pierre's gate with his hundred warriors behind him, Alisha's heart skipped a beat: Would Gray Eagle destroy her—or make his destiny her own?

FORBIDDEN ECSTASY (1014, $3.50)
Gray Eagle had promised Alisha his heart forever—nothing could keep him from her. But when Alisha woke to find her red-skinned lover gone, she felt abandoned and alone. Lost between two worlds, desperate and fearful of betrayal, Alisha, hungered for the return of her FORBIDDEN ECSTASY.

BRAZEN ECSTASY (1133, $3.50)
When Alisha is swept down a raging river and out of her savage brave's life, Gray Eagle must rescue his love again. But Alisha has no memory of him at all. And as she fights to recall a past love, another white slave woman in their camp is fighting for Gray Eagle.

TENDER ECSTACY (1212, $3.75)
Bright Arrow is committed to kill every white he sees—until he sets his eyes on ravishing Rebecca. And fate demands that he capture her, torment . . . and soar with her to the dizzying heights of TENDER ECSTACY.

STOLEN ECSTASY (1621, $3.95)
In this long-awaited sixth volume of the SAVAGE ECSTASY series, lovely Rebecca Kenny defies all for her true love, Bright Arrow. She fights with all her passion to be his lover—never his slave. Share in Rebecca and Bright Arrow's savage pleasure as they entwine in moments of STOLEN ECSTASY.

Available wherever paperbacks are sold, or order direct from the Publisher. Send cover price plus 50¢ per copy for mailing and handling to Zebra Books, Dept. 1314, 475 Park Avenue South, New York, N.Y. 10016. DO NOT SEND CASH.

GREAT WESTERNS
by Dan Parkinson

THE SLANTED COLT (1413, $2.25)
A tall, mysterious stranger named Kichener gave young Benjamin Franklin Blake a gift. It was a gun, a colt pistol, that had belonged to Ben's father. And when a cold-blooded killer vowed to put Ben six feet under, it was a sure thing that Ben would have to learn to use that gun — or die!

GUNPOWDER GLORY (1448, $2.50)
Jeremy Burke, breaking a deathbed promise to his pa, killed the lowdown Sutton boy who was the cause of his pa's death. But when the bullets started flying, he found there was more at stake than his own life as innocent people were caught in the crossfire of *Gunpowder Glory*.

BLOOD ARROW (1549, $2.50)
Randall Kerry returned to his camp to find his companion slaughtered and scalped. With a war cry as wild as the savages', the young scout raced forward with his pistol held high to meet them in battle.

BROTHER WOLF (1728, $2.95)
Only two men could help Lattimer run down the sheriff's killers — a stranger named Stillwell and an Apache who was as deadly with a Colt as he was with a knife. One of them would see justice done — from the muzzle of a six-gun.

CALAMITY TRAIL (1663, $2.95)
Charles Henry Clayton fled to the west to make his fortune, get married and settle down to a peaceful life. But the situation demanded that he strap on a six-gun and ride toward a showdown of gunpowder and blood that would send him galloping off to either death or glory on the . . . *Calamity Trail*.

Available wherever paperbacks are sold, or order direct from the Publisher. Send cover price plus 50¢ per copy for mailing and handling to Zebra Books, Dept. 1314, 475 Park Avenue South, New York, N.Y. 10016. DO NOT SEND CASH.